10 LUCKY THINGS THAT HAVE HAPPENED
TO ME SINCE I NEARLY GOT
HIT BY LIGHTNING

....

10 lucky things that have happened to me since I nearly got hit by lightning

Mary Hershey

WENDY
LAMB
BOOKS

Published by Wendy Lamb Books
an imprint of Random House Children's Books
a division of Random House, Inc.
New York

Wendy Lamb Books and colophon are trademarks of Random House, Inc.

Visit us on the Web! www.randomhouse.com/kids

Educators and librarians, for a variety of teaching tools, visit us at
www.randomhouse.com/teachers

Library of Congress Cataloging-in-Publication Data
Hershey, Mary.
10 lucky things that have happened to me since I nearly got hit by lightning /
Mary Hershey. — 1st ed.
p. cm.
Summary: Even though her father is in prison for embezzlement, ten-year-old Effie considers herself pretty lucky until her mother's old friend, Father Frank, comes to stay with them, Effie's friend Aurora decides to quit their Catholic school to attend public school, and her contrary sister begins to transform herself into "Saint Maxey."
ISBN 978-0-385-73541-4 (hardcover) —
ISBN 978-0-385-90522-0 (Gibraltar lib. bdg.)
[1. Identity—Fiction. 2. Priests—Fiction. 3. Catholic schools—Fiction.
4. Schools—Fiction. 5. Friendship—Fiction. 6. Interpersonal relations—Fiction.]
I. Title. II. Title: Ten lucky things that have happened to me since I nearly got hit by
lightning.
PZ7.H432428Aak 2008
[Fic]—dc22
2007030939

The text of this book is set in 11.5-point Italian Garamond.

Book design by Trish Parcell Watts

Printed in the United States of America

10 9 8 7 6 5 4 3 2 1

First Edition

For Kim and Diane,
the patron saints of best friendship,
with love and thanks forever
XO

Chapter 1

When you're the kid of a crook, and you live in a small town, you can count on three things. First off, nobody, except maybe your mom, is ever going to ask you to watch their purse. Second, kids are going to make fun of you. Particularly if they live on your street and remember watching the cops come drag your dad away in handcuffs. They just can't help making jokes. You're irresistible. And last, bad luck is going to follow you like a mangy old cat who's three meals behind. Even though I'm only ten, I've had a truckload of bad mojo in my life since my dad got sent to the Big House. I try not to dwell on it, though. My grandpa used to always say you get what you think about, whether you want it or not.

But since I nearly got shish-kebabbed by lightning at my school a couple of months ago, my whole life has changed.

Good luck is dumping on me like a blue norther. Like it finally found my address.

• • •

"Mom, make her shoot!" Maxey screamed from our driveway basketball court. "She's just standing there!"

"I'm *thinking* about it!" I hollered back.

"Effie, open your eyes!" Mom called.

I cocked an arm back like I was doing the shot put and fired it. The ball flew right out of bounds.

"Nice try, Effie!" my best friend Nit called, digging it out of the hedge.

Aurora Triboni, my other best friend, trotted up next to me. "That one was kind of better!" She slapped me on the back and nearly sent me flying.

Once I got my breath back, I sighed with pure happiness.

I live in Tyler Wash, Texas, with my big sister, Maxey, who is twelve and a bossaholic, and Coach Maloney, a very excellent high school coach and my mom. She's thirty-seven. The three of us have been on our own since they carted Dad off to prison a few years back. He was an embezzler, which isn't as bad as an ax murderer, but since most of the money he stole belonged to the people in our town, they weren't having any local parades in his honor.

"Time out!" Phil called. She's Maxey's best friend and Nit's older sister. She hurried over to her purse on the lawn.

"Get back here over here! You can't call a time-out," Maxey yelled.

"I need some gum! I'll just be a sec."

"You can't stop the game for gum!" Aurora shouted.

Mom blew her whistle. "Okay, let's take five, girls." She

took the ball from Nit and followed us to the lawn, where we collapsed. Except Aurora, who was stretching her calf against a tree.

"Two against three isn't fair, Mom," Maxey complained. She stabbed at her mouth with a lip gloss stick.

"Life isn't always fair, sugar. We'll switch teams after this. You and Effie will play Aurora, Phil, and Nit."

"*No!*" we both screamed.

My grandpa, who died last year, liked to say that Maxey and I got along as well as "two wildcats in a pillahcase." It was true, even though Mom was trying very hard to work on us. Like making us play basketball or touch football together every Saturday morning. If our friends were over, they had to play too. We all hated it, except Aurora, who loved sports, especially basketball. Just like Mom did. Maybe even more.

I could still hardly believe that just a few months ago, my best-friend count had been a big fat zero. Most girls are lucky to have one best friend. But I have two! First, there's Trinity Finch, whom I call Nit. At our school, St. Dominic's, a lot of kids still call her "HG," which is short for Holy Ghost. She got the name back in third grade, when she started hauling a big ol' Bible around with her. She wanted to read it cover to cover, she said, and it just took her a long time. I think it will probably take a long time before kids stop calling her HG.

Nit can be a tiny bit spooky because she sees things that most of us can't. Not like a fortune-teller who pulls things out of the blue, but Nit sees things that people usually miss. Like that time at the ribbon-cutting ceremony for the new children's library when Councilwoman Munding started talking really slow and slurry right in the middle her speech. People started whispering about it, but Nit hurried over with a cup of punch and gave her some. Nit figured she was diabetic and her blood sugar had gotten too low. She was right!

She says there are clues all around us if we really look for them. And she can find just about anything. In my school, people used to pray to St. Anthony if they lost something. Now they just ask Nit.

Aurora Triboni is my other best friend, and she is the biggest girl in fourth grade. I don't just mean the tallest. Not only does she have cool black hair under her arms, but all of a sudden, boobs. Nobody else in fourth grade has a chest. Donal, a boy in our class who just moved here from Ireland, said that Aurora had a "pair of puppies playing in her bloose," which is how he pronounces "blouse." Now the boys like to bark at her when she walks past them, even though our teacher told them to knock it off.

Phil dug her brush out of her pink and green sparkly purse. Maxey grabbed it. "Turn around," she said. "I'll do it." She started combing out the tangles in Phil's hair, soft and gentle, though ten seconds ago, she'd been all warrior princess. Hair does that to her. Makes her go all dreamy. She can't keep her hands off anyone's. Maxey has stick-straight white hair and I have crazy, curly red hair. The only way you can tell we're sisters is our round-the-clock fighting.

"Okay, girls," Mom said, passing around a big jug of water and cups. "Drink up. And let's do some stretching." She folded over at the waist, bobbing side to side, her dark ponytail swishing. Mom is nearly middle-aged, but she's really pretty, even without her makeup.

We all kind of ignored her. Except Aurora, who thought Mom hung the moon. She'd even started wearing her hair in the same kind of ponytail, too.

Nit pulled off her Notre Dame cap and poured water over her head. "Oh, that feels good." Nit is skinny; she likes to read more than do sports. Since we've become best friends, though, she doesn't look so pasty. She's even grown a few freckles on her nose.

"Uh-oh," Maxey said. "Here they come! The Comstock Lane Comedians."

She meant the Turner brothers. They're older boys— sixteen, seventeen, and nineteen. They all chew tobacco, rarely mind their mother, and are trying to grow mustaches— wispy-looking things. They'd all been outside playing the day the cops came for my dad. I think it was the highlight of their sorry little lives.

Mom gave them a friendly wave, though they didn't deserve it. They used to dump trash on our lawn and once even spray painted a bad word on our garage.

She blew her whistle. "On the court, girls. Just ignore them."

Aurora squinted their way. "Oh, man, Chip is with them."

"Your big brother?" Nit asked.

"Yeah, he thinks they're cool. What a bunch of losers. He's supposed to be at an Eagle Scout meeting."

Mom tossed the ball to her. "Okay, Effie and Maxey— home team. Phil, Aurora, and Nit—visitors. Let's play ball!"

Aurora shot the ball to Phil, who had twirled around at the sound of whistling. It hit her hard in the back of the head. "Ow!" she screamed. "Foul!"

"I'm on your team! I can't foul you!" Aurora yelled. "Would you pay attention?"

Maxey scooped up the ball and ran for the basket. Aurora went at her like a tank.

The boys hooted from the street. "Yo, Maxey! Let's see what you got!"

Aurora covered her like a dark cloud—top, bottom, side, every which way Maxey could move.

I waved my arms at her. "Over here! Throw it to me!"

She ignored me and ground her shoulder into Aurora, trying to move her.

"Hey, sis!" Chip yelled at her. "Watch your wallet. The little one will sneak it out before you know it!"

Maxey elbowed Aurora in the gut, then turned and hurled the ball into the street at them. Mom leapt in and grabbed it just in time.

The Turner boys hooted and yelled. "Bring it on, girl, bring it *on*!"

"Move out, boys," Mom said, her voice even but steely.

"Chip, I'm going to kill you!" Aurora shouted.

Mom grabbed Aurora by the back of the shirt as she raced by.

"Lunch!" she called, taking Aurora by the shoulders and spinning her around.

"In the house, all of you!"

"Whatcha havin'?" the youngest Turner boy yelled. "Con salad?"

"Dude!" his brother said, slapping him on the back of the head. "Get some new material, will ya?"

"C'mon, let's get going, guys. This scene is dead," Chip said.

"No kidding," the biggest brother added.

Mom stood on the porch until she got us all inside. Used to be we could hardly get rid of the Turners when they set their minds on pestering us. They'd ring our doorbell over and over, or have tobacco-juice-spitting contests right in front of our house. But in the last few months, we didn't see them as much.

"Let's eat," Phil said to Maxey. "I have to get home."

They pulled out Mom's platter of sandwiches.

I watched the Turners from the kitchen window until they turned the corner toward town. Gone! My good luck just didn't let up. I grabbed a pencil and went over to my list on the fridge. I wrote in number seven.

EFFIE'S LIST OF LUCKY THINGS

1. My principal lets me go have hot chocolate in her office.
2. I found one of my grandpa's diamond cuff links in the couch. Mom let me keep it and it's very ritzy.
3. I went to the doctor for a checkup and she forgot to give me my tetanus shot.
4. I left my library book on the roof of our car and we drove off. Someone found it in the street and turned it in before the due date.
5. I won a cordless power drill at the hardware store.
6. My goldfish, Bubba, just had his first birthday and is my longest-lasting fish ever!
7. The Turner boys are getting bored with us!

Chapter 2

"Yard work!" Maxey yelled.

"Yep, yard work," Mom said. "The back looks like a wilderness preserve. And some darn gopher is out there trying to build an underground railway."

"But, Mom," Maxey complained, "why do I have to work in the yard, and Effie gets to have her friends stay?"

"Because it's her turn. You had Phil over all last weekend. Tell you what, Max. You help me trap that gopher, and I'll let you stay up till eleven tonight."

"Can I watch wrestling?"

"Deal! Now let's get out of the girls' hair. They're going to make valentines and we'll just be in the way."

Maxey gave me a triumphant look as she headed out to the kitchen with Mom.

"She's a piece of work," Nit said, dumping her backpack on the dining-room table. She unzipped it and pulled out a big plastic tub. She popped off the lid and took a deep sniff. "Perfect!" she said. "I brought garlic mac 'n' cheese 'n' olives to share."

I fanned my face as the smell headed toward me. "Nit, how much garlic did you put in that?"

"Enough to keep us vampire-free for days," she said, plopping it down in the middle of the table.

Aurora and I shot a glance at each other. Nit was still nose deep in *The Complete History of Vampires*. It was an even bigger book than the Bible. Everything was about vampires right now. Aurora and I didn't really believe in them, but Nit believed enough for the three of us.

Aurora opened her gym bag and pulled out an enormous box of store-bought cupcakes with giant frosting tops. You could always count on Aurora to bring the best snacks for Girls' Pot Lunch.

We'd invented this after about a month of being best friends. I craved anything sweet, fattening, and junky because my mom was a health-food nut. Aurora was the only girl in her big family, and she was the head cook at her house, since her parents worked all the time. The Triboni kids ate a lot of heat-up foods like pizza and frozen dinners. Aurora was always hungry for something homemade. And Nit always brought something very interesting to eat.

I ducked into the kitchen and grabbed the plate of sandwiches. Phil and Maxey had already eaten. I set it down on the dining-room table.

Aurora's cell phone jingled, and we all looked at her bag, horrified.

"Oh, no!" I said.

"Cross your fingers," she said with a big sigh. Her mom made her carry a cell phone in case they needed her to come home, or had to ask her where the diaper-rash cream was. Aurora had a lot of brothers, but they were useless about household stuff. Unless maybe some mice got in the house. They all had BB guns and liked to shoot things.

She looked at the incoming number. "Not my folks. Hellooo?"

We waited.

"How did you get this number?" she said, her dark eyebrows forming a V.

"Don't ever call me again!" She snapped the phone shut. Her face red, she sat down hard, poked her finger into the top of a cupcake, and shoveled a load of frosting into her mouth.

"Who was *that*?" I asked.

Aurora leaned back in her chair and crossed her arms over her chest. "I hate this."

"Hate what?"

"That I look different now and boys are acting like idiots about it."

"Was that a *boy*?" I'd never gotten a call from a boy.

"Not just any boy. I'm betting that was none other than Himself," Nit said.

Aurora sunk lower in her chair. "Yeah. He said he was calling for 'someone else,' who wanted to know what my favorite Valentine candy is."

"*Who* wants to know that?" I nearly shrieked.

"Booger Boy," Aurora said.

"But he's in sixth grade! And he's so disgusting!"

"I know!" She started on another cupcake. "That's what makes this all so creepy. Somebody has been leaving me these dumb notes in my desk, and I'm sure it's him. Last week, he tried to give me a cookie from his lunch bag. Like I'd eat anything he touched!"

"I wonder who the 'someone else' might be," Nit puzzled.

Aurora shook her head. "I bet he's making that up. He's the one that wants to know!"

"But how'd he get your number?" I passed the sandwiches.

"I dunno," she said, rolling her basketball under her feet. "One of my stupid brothers probably sold it to him."

Nit lifted the lid off her sandwich and pressed a glob of garlicky macaroni into it. "He's a very determined kid."

"Yeah, I know! Mom told me to just ignore him, but it's not working!"

"How'd you know it was Booger Boy?" I asked Nit.

"Look at her! He's the only kid that makes her turn that red in the face."

"How come you didn't tell us about this before, Aurora? We're your best friends," I said.

She lifted her shoulders, then dropped them. "It's embarrassing! It's bad enough that I'm getting an early visit from the Puberty Fairy. Having Booger Boy like me makes me an official freak. He probably wants to get me into his Amazing Marvels and Gross-Out Show."

"I'd like to see him try!" I said. "No way!"

"We need a plan," Nit said. "There's three of us and just one of him."

I frowned. "But how do you get a boy to stop liking you?" That certainly had never been a discussion I'd overheard during my eavesdropping on Maxey. It was always the other way around.

"There must be a lot of ways," Nit said. "I'll start doing some research!"

Aurora ripped the paper liner off her cupcake. She sighed hard. "Couldn't I just whoop him good?"

"Hey!" I said. "I have an idea. You have to have really fresh breath to make a boy like you. Maxey goes through about three packs of breath mints a day. Why don't you try for stinky breath? You could eat a bunch of Nit's garlic mac 'n' cheese."

"Effie," Nit said, "you can't fight love with bad breath. If that were possible, the human race would have never survived."

Aurora propped her chin in her fist. "What do you fight love with?"

We all bit into our sandwiches and chewed for a minute.

Then Nit said, "You don't fight it. But you can out-smart it."

Chapter 3

We had a hard time getting Aurora to concentrate on making valentines for our classmates after Booger Boy called. Marcus had gotten the nickname because he had a big snot collection he'd pasted on the outside of his old lunch box, with "From" labels and everything. Principal Obermeyer wouldn't let him bring it to school anymore, so kids had to go to his house if they wanted to see it. He collected lots of disgusting things and made kids pay money to see them.

We wanted to make copies of one valentine from all three of us. Nit had drawn a Valentine vampire. Aurora wanted a basketball on the front, and I wanted hearts with pasted-on pink buttons that I'd saved from an old church dress. We ended up with a pink Valentine vampire with red fangs, who was bouncing a basketball. The inside read:

Hoop you get baskets of sweets
on St. Valentine's Day.
Your friends, Effie Maloney, Aurora Triboni,
and Trinity Finch

Then we glued a pink button on the envelope, with a string to tie it closed, just to make it fancier. I didn't know how I'd stand waiting until Friday to give them out at school. But I'd have six whole days when I could look at them myself.

I made a very special one just from me for Principal Obermeyer, who was on a long trip called a sabbatical. It's sort of like a vacation for teachers, but you have to study while you are on it. I couldn't wait until she got back. She left Sister Emmanuel in charge. I doubted even Sister's mother would want to send her a valentine. No one could ever remember seeing Sister Emmanuel smile. She had a mean old dog, too.

Nit and Aurora left around two-thirty, and I was cleaning up our mess when Maxey came flying back into the house. She and Mom had been outside the whole afternoon chasing the gopher and hosing out his tunnels. Once Maxey got her mind behind something, you could hardly get her off it.

"Can I borrow Bubba?" she asked, nearly out of breath.

"What do you need a goldfish for?"

"Gopher bait!"

"*Whaat?*"

"I need something better to get that gopher into the trap. Mom put lettuce and cheese out, but he's not going for it. He needs something alive and kicking."

"NO!"

"Oh, come on, you've had him forever. He's probably ready to croak. I'll buy you a fresh one."

"Stay away from Bubba!"

"Oh, fine!" She wiped her dirty hands on her jeans. She reached over to pick up one of my cards, and I grabbed it away just in time.

"I only want to look," she said. "Mom says strong teams have to learn to share, remember?"

I hustled my cards into a pile. I knew she'd make fun of them. "Where's Mom?"

"Outside. She's been on her cell phone for about an hour! I had to do all the work."

"Who's she talking to?" I asked. Mom was not a phone person at all.

Maxey edged closer to my stack of cards. "Dunno. She's mostly listening. Whoever it is has a lot on their mind." She spied my pile of buttons. "Buttons on your valentines? That is so preschool!"

"Hey! I know something you don't know!" I tried to distract her.

"In your dreams, Effie."

"Oh, yeah?" I said. "Guess what very disgusting boy is in love with Aurora?"

She grabbed a leftover cupcake and studied the top. Looking for cooties, I imagined. She sniffed it. "And why would I care about your freakish friend?"

"Because the boy is in your class!" I said, triumphant.

Maxey licked a ring around the top. "All the boys in my class are obsessed with her. It's her boobs. That's all. Nothing for her to get a big head about."

"She doesn't have a big head! And they shouldn't be look-ing," I said. "It's not like she can help it."

"She'll get her period now for sure," Maxey continued. "Breasts are a sign that your period is on its way."

I knew she was right. Nit and I had a bet going about when Aurora would start. "I know why she's maturing so early," Maxey said in her Miss Science Pants voice.

I couldn't wait to hear this.

"It's from chickens. Farmers give their chickens hormones to plump up their breasts so when they sell them to the supermarket, they make more money. Aurora is eating way too much chicken. You better tell her to go easy on it and get her mother to buy the hormone-free kind," Maxey warned. "Or she might get even bigger."

I shook my head. "Did you just make that up?"

"Nope, it's scientifically proven," she said. "If you don't believe me, ask her how often she eats chicken."

"*We* eat chicken."

Maxey smoothed her shirt down over her chest. "Not enough."

• • •

It had been a long time since I'd been so excited about Valentine's Day. I made cards for both Nit and Aurora with very fancy buttons. One belonged to a good sweater of Maxey's, and if she ever figured that out, I'd be in such trou-ble. I took one off the very bottom, not like in the middle or anything. She hardly ever buttoned up her sweater anyway.

Most years, I usually got a valentine from my teacher, one from Nit, and maybe some from a few other kids whose mothers made them give one to everybody. And I always held my breath when the teacher told the story about how St. Valentine invented the tradition of giving out cards when he was in prison, in case someone asked if I got a card from my dad in the slammer.

Mr. Giles, my fourth-grade teacher, was British and talked just like Prince Charles, only a lot louder. He had hair growing inside his ears, and I think it made it hard for him to hear. He made us wait until last period to pass out our valentines and have our special treats from the nuns. They always baked us big heart-shaped cookies. It was so hard to wait!

Aurora had been kind of tense all day, like she was worried that Booger Boy was going to show up with a box of candy. By the time lunch and our last break was over and he hadn't paid a lick of attention to her, she started to relax. She'd painted a big red heart on her basketball. I was wearing bright red socks even though they didn't match our itchy black-and-green plaid uniforms. Nit had painted her fingernails red, black, and purple.

At three o'clock on the dot, a half hour before school let out, there was a knock on our classroom door. Mr. Giles looked up from drawing a picture of the Panama Canal. He was crazy for that canal.

It was fifteen minutes too early for our treats.

Kayla Quintana, Aurora's ex–best friend, shot out of her seat. Aurora had finally figured out that creeps like Kayla don't want best friends, they want hostages. Aurora wised up and called it quits with her a few weeks back. "I'll get it, Mr. Giles," Kayla said, even though it wasn't her turn to answer the door this week.

Sister Mary Michael came marching in, followed by the entire St. Dominic's choir, which was twenty kids from all different grades. Everyone liked Sister Mary Michael. She was the one who showed the puberty movies to kids, even though it made her face turn pink and sweaty. We figured she had to be about ninety. She didn't teach anymore, but she liked to work the projectors, raise money for starving children, and lead the choir.

Mr. Giles looked puzzled as the choir lined up in three rows, ready to belt out a tune. All the choir kids were holding one red rose in their hands.

"Sister?" he asked. "I wasn't told there would be music today. I haven't finished my lesson yet."

She waved a hand at him. "We won't take long, Mr. Giles. We've been hired to sing a song to one of your students."

"Oh?" he said.

We all looked around at each other. Wow! A singing valentine.

Sister pulled her small pitch pipe from the inside of her nun's habit and blew a note. Then she lifted her hand to the choir to begin.

> *"Ain't she sweet!*
> *With her super size-ten feet!*
> *Now, I tell you very confidentially,*
> *Triboni is so sweet."*

Kids whipped around in their seats to look at Aurora and started to laugh. Nit and I sent a look to each other. Uh-oh. Aurora stared straight ahead, like she'd been frozen.

> *"Ain't she fine!*
> *I see her dribbling all the time!*

Now, I tell you very confidentially,
Wish she were mine!"

I could see Aurora's jaw muscle working.

"Ain't she true!
Now, my name's not Sam or Sue.
Well, I'll tell you very confidentially,
You'll never guess from who!"

Aurora bolted from her desk. The choir members tried to hand their roses to her, but she knocked them away and shoved the door open.

Smack into Marcus.

Chapter 4

"**Y**ou MAGGOT!" she screamed.

We all scrambled out of our desks. Aurora had Booger Boy by the front of the shirt and was shaking him. "I warned you to leave me alone!"

He tried to wrench her hands off of him. "*Whaat?* I'm coming for choir!"

"Children!" Mr. Giles barked. "Back to your seats at once!"

"I'm WARNING you!" She gave Marcus another shake.

"Miss Triboni! I'm warning YOU! Take your hands off him right now!" Mr. Giles shouted.

"Let go, Aurora," Donal yelled. "He's bollocks!"

Aurora chased Marcus out the door.

Mr. Giles herded all of us back into the room, even the choir kids. "Sister Mary Michael! Go get Sister Emmanuel!"

We all rushed to the window. Aurora was pushing him around the blacktop. She was still screaming.

Nit squeezed in beside me. "Effie, we've got to do something!"

"I know, but *what*?"

Mr. Giles ran outside, grabbed Aurora around the waist, and pulled. She wouldn't let go.

"Now she's done it!" Kayla said. "Here comes Sister Emmanuel." She threw open the window so we could hear better.

"Young lady!" Sister Emmanuel shouted as she approached. "Stop this right now!"

"Make HIM stop!" Aurora shouted. "This is his fault!"

"I'm not doing anything, Sister," Booger Boy panted. "She's gone crazy." He grunted as Aurora tightened her grip on him.

"Let him go this INSTANT, Miss Triboni! Hold her, Mr. Giles!" She tried to wedge her body between Aurora and Booger Boy.

Sister peeled Aurora's fingers off his shirt. Aurora lost her balance and started to fall. At the last second, she grabbed Sister's habit.

All of us squealed in horror as we watched Aurora hit the ground, pulling Sister's head veil down with her.

Sister Emmanuel's hands flew to her head. Too late.

"Holy show!" Donal exclaimed. "The old bird's wearing rollers!"

• • •

Even though it was already past three-thirty, and time to go home, Mr. Giles kept us all in our classroom. He said everyone needed to calm down and finish our lesson. To be honest, I think it was Mr. Giles who needed to be calmed down. He was all rumpled and had torn the knee out of his good pants. He kept talking about the Panama Canal, like anyone could concentrate on that. Mr. Giles said that he'd drive anyone home who missed the bus. Me and Donal were the only ones who rode it to school every day. Other kids had parents or car pools. Some walked if they lived close enough.

After the pileup outside, Sister Emmanuel had grabbed her veil from Aurora and draped it back over her head all crooked. She'd leaned over Aurora, poked a finger in her face, and said something we couldn't hear. Then she'd brushed off her habit and stormed off to the office. She turned once and barked, "Sister Mary Michael! Follow me."

Booger Boy tried to give Aurora a hand up, and she slapped it away. Mr. Giles sent him to his homeroom and led Aurora back to class. We'd all leapt back to our seats, and the choir kids had split. The story would be all over school in three minutes flat.

I'd been trying to get Aurora's attention ever since she came back in, but she wouldn't look up from her book.

I had a terrible feeling we weren't going to get our special Valentine cookies today.

Mr. Giles finished his lesson and gave out our homework assignment. Then he told us we could pass out our cards, but all the fun had been sucked right out of it. We handed them out, but nobody except Donal seemed very excited about it.

"This is grand!" he shouted as he collected more and more valentines. He was giving out very babyish store-bought ones that had kitties and cowboys on them—the kind that you could buy at Earline's Eighty-Eight Cents Store. But we knew he didn't know any better. I had quite a stack on my desk, but I just scooped them into my backpack to look at later. Aurora left hers on her desk and took off the minute Mr. Giles dismissed us. I started to go after her, but Nit pulled the back of my sweater.

"Leave her alone. We'll talk later."

Donal and I helped Mr. Giles erase all the boards while the other kids packed up and left. There were a lot of giggly whispers going on about why Sister Emmanuel had her hair in curlers. Kayla said maybe she had a secret Valentine's date that night.

Mr. Giles held the door open until everyone filed out, and then he turned off the lights and locked the door. He put us in the backseat of his van and made sure we were strapped in. Donal wanted to ride in the front, but Mr. Giles said the back was safer. It made me a little nervous that we hadn't even left the parking lot yet and he was already thinking about us crashing.

"Bloody class wheels ya got 'ere!" Donal said.

"We don't say 'bloody,' Donal," Mr. Giles reminded him, as he did nearly every day. Nit said it was kind of like a swearword, and educated Irish and English people didn't say it in public. When Donal came to our school, nobody could understand what he was saying. Nit studied up on Irish slang and stuff so she could interpret for him.

"Sorry about your torn pants, Mr. Giles," I offered from the backseat.

"Ya have a missus at home to fix 'em?" Donal asked. "Or maybe yer oul ma?"

I gave him a sideways stare. "Do you think you have to be a girl to sew? Boys and men can learn how to do those things, too," I said. I'd learned this from my mom at our weekly Team Meetings. She didn't want us growing up thinking we had to take care of men or do all the housework. Though in our house we did have to do all the chores because we didn't have any men to help. About the only time I minded that was on chore day.

"Point well taken, Effie," Mr. Giles said. "I'm quite certain I can repair them."

"Don't get cheesed off," Donal said to me.

I shot him a look. "This is all your fault, you know!"

"What the divil you wagging 'bout?"

"The boys didn't start treating Aurora different until you made that stupid comment about the puppies running loose in her 'bloose'!"

Mr. Giles looked up into his rearview mirror at Donal. "Did you say that to her?"

Donal squirmed under his seat belt. "Yeah," he said. "I shouldn't've. I was just twistin' hay with the lads."

"Yeah, well," I said, "now they're all barking at her constantly, and they can't stop looking at her you-know-whats!"

"I had nothin' to do with what Boger Boy did! He's on his own with that sorry mess."

I turned as far away as I could from him and stared out the window.

"I could give a go at fixin' it with the lads," he said.

I kept my shoulder pointed toward him.

"Snobby weather back here," he said with a sigh.

Mr. Giles cleared his throat. He did that a lot. "Donal, your remark about Aurora was ungentlemanly, and unkind. I'm sure it has caused her a great deal of embarrassment. You are keenly aware of how hard it is to be different from your classmates."

I peeked at Donal. Now he was looking out his window, and I could see his ears were red.

"In this country," Mr. Giles continued, "we don't make rude comments or stare at a person's private parts. Those things are holy, and not to be profaned."

Now my ears were turning red. I sure hoped Mr. Giles wasn't going to keep talking about private parts in front of Donal and me. Sometimes he'd get on a topic and wouldn't get off it. I held my breath.

"Yes, sir," Donal said. "Aurora's a fine bit of stuff. Meant no 'arm to her."

Now it was my turn to have Mr. Giles look at me in the mirror. "Effeline, I'll speak to the boys in the class and let them know that I won't tolerate them making fun of Aurora. We want all the boys and girls at St. Dominic's to feel safe and accepted. It's one of the advantages of going to a private school. Children don't have to be harassed by hooligans and rowdies."

"Thank you, sir," I said.

But I didn't have a lot of hope. Mr. Giles knew an awful lot about math, science, and the Panama Canal, but when it came to kids, he didn't have a clue.

Chapter 5

The next afternoon Nit and Aurora were lying on their stomachs on the matted pink carpet in Aurora's bedroom when I got there. They looked like a girl version of David and Goliath. Nit was the smart, puny one, and Aurora was the giant. Only, she wasn't scary at all, except if you were playing dodgeball against her.

I gave a happy sigh and dumped my backpack on the bed. I loved coming to the Tribonis'. There were no sisters here, and Aurora had her own princess bedroom all to herself. And there were lots of sugary snacks and no rules about them. I dropped down cross-legged on the rug. They had Nit's vampire book open. I dug my hand into the megabag of chocolate chips they were eating. At Aurora's, you could eat her mother's chocolate chips for baking right out of the bag and no one cared.

"Check it out!" Aurora said, stabbing at a picture with her finger. "That one looks like Sister Emmanuel."

Nit studied it. "Effie, do you think this vampire looks like Sister?"

"Well, he's all in black like her, but"—I pointed at his shoes—"no cowboy boots."

Nit laughed. "She's a cowgirl, that's for sure. And she'd never make it as a vampire. Couldn't sneak up on the dead."

"Boots look stupid with her habit," Aurora said. "None of the other nuns wear them."

"None of the other nuns were former rodeo barrel racers, either," Nit said. "And her dad is a Texas Ranger, you know. Legend has it that the babies of Texas Rangers come out of the chute wearing boots."

I spied Aurora's cell phone on her dresser. "Hey! Did Booger Boy call you about what happened yesterday?"

"No, and he better not!" She grabbed a tennis ball and threw it against the wall. "Sister called last night, though, and gave my folks an earful. She banned me from Angel Scout Camp in Rockdale next month. And I'm suspended on Monday."

"Oh, no!" I wailed. The three of us had been talking about going to camp together for weeks.

"What's going to happen to Booger Boy?" Nit asked.

"My dad wanted to know that, too. Sister Emmanuel told him that as far as she was concerned, Marcus hadn't done anything wrong, and had shown 'remarkable restraint' while I shoved him all over the playground!"

"But what about the singing valentine?" Nit asked. "He mortally embarrassed you. Doesn't that count for something?"

"Apparently not. Sister Emmanuel said that giving valentines to fellow students was a long-standing tradition at St. Dom's, and *if* he had been the one to send it, he'd found a very creative way to have it delivered. Sister said he kept denying it was from him. And there's no proof since I guess the song and donation had come without any name on it."

"Principal Obermeyer never should have put Sister E in charge when she left on her trip," I said. "She would have at least suspended Booger Boy, too. This is so unfair."

Aurora dropped down on her back. "My dad was really ticked last night. I heard him talking to Mom after we all went to bed. He said he didn't know why they were spending good money on a private school being run by such fools. He said *I* showed 'remarkable restraint' for not just hauling off and clocking Marcus. Said he wouldn't have been a bit mad if I had. That's not all he said—" Aurora stopped.

A tiny shiver raced up my back. I had a bad feeling. "What?"

"He said he thought they should let me transfer to public school if I wanted."

"Public school!" I yelled.

Aurora bit down on her bottom lip. "I don't fit in at St. Dominic's anymore."

"Of course you do! You're just about the most popular girl in our class."

"Only because I'm the tallest. Now I'm turning into the freakiest. Besides, public school has better sports," she said. "Dad told Mom that if I wanted to get into a good college, I'd need a sports scholarship. Eventually I'll have to transfer to public school so I can be on some real teams and get scouted."

"But you're only in fourth grade. Couldn't you wait until, like, tenth grade to transfer?" I looked at Nit.

"Do you want to go to public school, Aurora?" Nit asked.

"Of course she doesn't want to go," I jumped in. "She wants to stay with us!"

"Aurora?" Nit asked again, softer.

"I do want to stay. I haven't ever had two such good friends in my whole life!"

Nit nodded. "Me either."

My throat burned. "Me too."

We were silent, shy about how we felt about each other.

I swallowed. "I don't know what I'd do without the two of you. I don't want anything to ruin it."

"But, Ef," Aurora said, "don't you think we could still be best friends if I went to public school? We could still call each other every day and hang out all weekend."

"It would change everything. Best friends go to the same school!"

Nit nodded. "I think Effie's probably right. We could still be friends, of course, but you'd make new ones and they'd want you to call them, too, and come over on the weekends."

Aurora blew out a big breath. "I guess you're right."

"Okay, then," I said. "You have to stay at least until we graduate from ninth grade. Look, we can fix this. That's what best friends do. Stick together when things get hard."

Aurora smiled, but the smile never made it up into her eyes.

I knew what I had to do. Fix Booger Boy's wagon. Fix it good.

Chapter 6

I love Sunday mornings at my house when we've already gone to church the night before. Mom lets us sleep in. And instead of our regular alarm clock, we wake up to the smell of macadamia nut French toast or banana pecan pancakes. If it's Maxey's turn, we get the pancakes, but it was my week, and my rumbling stomach woke me up at 9:37. I turned to look over at Maxey's bed, but she was already up and gone.

I sat up and sniffed. Nothing cooking yet, which seemed kind of weird. I threw off the covers and ran down to investigate. Maybe Maxey had done something bad, and Mom was superbusy punishing her. I didn't want to miss any of that.

As I came down the stairs, I heard talking, but one voice didn't belong.

I swung open the door to the kitchen. There was a *man* sitting in our breakfast nook. We never had any of those in our house.

Mom was running around making coffee, and smiling like she does only when her basketball team goes to the state championships.

Maxey was staring at him bug-eyed, as if he'd just arrived in a spaceship. She must have woken up to the smell of man and hurried right down.

Maxey loved men, all kinds: teachers, our plumber, the postman, even the guy who came and sprayed for bugs. She reminded me of a spider spinning a web around them to try to make them stay.

"Good morning, Ef! I'm so glad you're up," Mom said, sounding way too happy. "I want you to meet Father Francisco Avila, my dear old friend from college. You've heard me talk about him for years. Father, this is Effeline, my youngest."

He gave me a big grin, and I could see why Maxey was in a near coma. He was what she and Phil call a "hotcake." But you have to be twelve to like that sort of thing.

He held out his hand. "Please just call me Frank. We met once a very long time ago."

Mom looked at him, then at me. "It's Father Avila, Effie."

I didn't care if he was Pope Avila. He seemed nice, and it was sort of interesting to have a man visitor. But I hoped we weren't going to have to sit around all morning. And I sure hoped Mom wouldn't ask him to hear our holy confessions later. I had a couple of things that I definitely didn't want Mom's old friend Frank to know about.

"I haven't seen such beautiful red hair since—" he started.

"Do you need some more sugar, Father?" Maxey interrupted, digging a spoon deep into the sugar bowl. "We have plenty, and there's more in the cupboard. We have brown sugar and organic, too."

"No thanks, Maxine," he said, putting his hand over his cup.

I looked up at the clock. It was near ten and I had very important plans. There wasn't any breakfast cooking, which was not a good sign. Usually by now the kitchen was a mess and Mom had the Dixie Chicks playing.

Pretty Girl, my grandpa's cat, who is very old and always cranky, came into the kitchen and growled. She stood in front of the fridge and twitched her tail. Even Pretty Girl knew it was Sunday and time for our special breakfast. Mom always lets her lick the egg bowl.

"Can I crack the eggs for the French toast, Mom?" I asked. "It's my turn," I added before Maxey jumped in. If I wanted to do it, Maxey would automatically want it, too. It didn't matter how dumb a thing it was. I shot a look at her, but she was flapping her white-blond eyelashes at Father Avila.

"Hey! Let me cook, will you?" he said. "I'd love to make breakfast for the three of you."

Mom started to protest, but he was already buried deep in the fridge. Before we knew it, he was cracking eggs one-handed. "Have you ever tried New Mexican Toast?" He whisked the eggs like a real pro.

"No! But we'd love to!" Maxey said.

She would have agreed to Chopped Toenail Toast if it meant he would stay for breakfast.

He looked over at me and Mom. "You two game?" he asked. Mom gave him a big thumbs-up, and I said, "Y-E-S, Father."

He winked at me. "I'll need an assistant. Effie, can you help?"

Maxey fired a murderous look my way. This could be fun.

He rubbed his hands together, looking happier than priests usually do. "I'll need some chili powder, cocoa powder, a shot of spicy tomato juice if you've got it, and if there are any green chilies or fresh peppers around, we're in business."

Maxey and I crashed into each other at the fridge. Our hips and shoulders ground together so hard you could hear the bones.

She growled. "*I'm* getting the tomato juice. *You* get the other stuff."

She tried to pry my fingers off the handle. When she pulled with all her might, I let go, and my hand hit her in the face. By accident, of course.

Maxey turned purplish and normally would have killed me on the spot. If she had, it would have been a good thing we had a priest in the kitchen because then Father could have given me Last Rites. She turned to holler for Mom but stopped.

There were Mom and Father Avila standing real close at the stove, both smiling.

What might it be like to have a mom and a dad cooking for us on Sunday mornings? I couldn't even imagine having two adults looking out for you, taking you places, and talking to you about stuff. I didn't need it, and I wouldn't like it.

"Look how happy she is," Maxey whispered. "She needs a boyfriend, or a husband."

"No, she doesn't," I muttered. There wasn't room for anyone else in our house.

Our car was too small for two adults and two growing girls. Plus, we had only three bikes, three dining-room chairs that weren't broken, and three of the good iced-tea glasses.

We were a threesome. We balanced. When we voted on things, we never had to worry about a tie. And it must be God's favorite number because of the whole Trinity thing He worked out.

"I bet he's the one she's been on the phone with all week!" Maxey said, close to my ear.

I bit my lip and kept looking at them. It was like they'd forgotten we were still in the room. Maxey was probably right. Mom had been on the phone an awful lot this week. Whenever we asked her who she was talking to, she'd say, "Just an old friend."

Hmmm. I was betting dollars to doughnuts that I was going to have to sit on the squeaky folding chair during breakfast since I was the smallest. Oh, well, he'd be gone soon.

Shows you how much I know.

Chapter 7

"Girls!" Mom yelled up the stairs and blew her whistle. "Come on down. Huddle up!"

Mom and Father Avila had gone for a run after they gorged on New Mexican Toast. It wasn't bad, but there weren't any macadamia nuts in it. I ate just one-half of a piece.

After they'd finished the dishes and left, Maxey got on the phone with Phil. She told her that Father Avila was "a drop-dead gorgeous piece of beefcake." They were screeching, and I couldn't help hearing the whole conversation, both ends.

I was in the upstairs bathroom trying to tame my hair into a braid when Mom got back.

"Is Father still here, Mom?" Maxey gasped after she sprinted down the stairs and just about rolled me over.

"He'll be back later for supper," Mom said. We crowded around her on the couch.

She reached under her tank top and pulled off the heart-rate monitor that she runs with. She tossed it on the table and gave us a long look. "Girls, Father Avila is going to stay with us for a while. . . ."

Maxey jumped into a cheerleader victory pose. "YES!"

"Why?" I had a very bad feeling.

"It's a bit complicated," Mom said. "But, I do want you to understand some of what this is about. Frank—I mean, *Father*—said I could tell you."

We both waited, already pretty stunned at the idea of a man roommate.

"He's having a bit of a spiritual crisis," Mom said, in her most private voice. "He needs a short time-out from the priesthood so he can think. I've offered him a place to stay while he does that."

"But we don't have any room!" I said. "Where will he stay?"

"You are so selfish, Effie!" Maxey said. "He can have my bed, Mom. I'll sleep on the floor next to him. Or I can sleep out in the car!"

"That won't be necessary," she said. "He can sleep on the pull-out couch in my office."

"Why can't he stay over at the church with our priests?" I asked. "Their place is huge. They have a housekeeper and everything."

Mom hesitated and then said, "Girls, I need to know that I can trust the both of you with something private, for this family's ears only."

Maxey moved in a little closer to Mom. My bad feeling grew warts. But we both nodded.

Mom continued. "Father Avila doesn't want anyone to know where he is—for now, at least."

"You mean, he's a runaway?" I was shocked.

"How romantic!" Maxey slumped back on the couch.

"Girls! This is serious. I need you to give me your word that for as long as Father is with us, we will keep this in the family."

"Why doesn't he want anyone to know where he is, Mom? Did he do something bad?" I asked.

"No, absolutely not. Father Avila is one of the finest men and priests I've ever known. In fact, the Church wants to move him up. They have their eye on him for a very important leadership position."

Maxey gasped. "I bet they want him to be the Pope, don't they?"

"Maxey, slow down!" Mom said. "You can't go from priest to Pope."

"But he might be someday, and then we could go visit him in the Vatican. And maybe we could be in a parade with him and ride in that little Pope-mobile he's got. Phil would *die* of jealousy."

Mom gave Maxey her hand signal for time-out. "I need you to listen, girls. He's getting pressure to leave the work he loves helping people, for a desk job high up in the Church. They are grooming him to become a bishop. And that's not where his heart is. But obedience is one of the vows that he took."

"I think he should be obedient and go back right away," I said.

Mom gave me a long look. "Father Frank is one of my dearest friends, and he needs our help. When your father went to prison, Frank was there for me. He helped me with the difficult decision to get a divorce. Now he needs a private place to think, and a friend he can trust. If his monsignor and the bishop find out where he is, they'll insist he come back. They want to move him to Boston, and he wants to continue his work with the immigrants near the border towns. He speaks Spanish and doesn't mind living very simply. He feels most needed there."

"I'll need some new pajamas," Maxey said, her voice dreamy.

"How are we supposed to hide a whole grown man, Mom?" I asked. "Somebody is going to see him. He's way bigger than Anne Frank!"

"Do you think he might decide not to be a priest at all?" Maxey asked. She shot up straight. "Is *that* what his crisis is?"

"You know all you need to know, young lady." She turned to me. "Effie, we don't need to hide him, but let's just keep the fact that he is a priest between us. I want to protect his privacy. And so people don't come by looking for his counsel or help. We want him to have a nice rest with us. While he's here, we'll just tell people he's an old college buddy of mine. That's completely true. And, I'm going to give you both permission to call him Frank—just in this emergency situation."

"I'm going to call him Frankie," Maxey said. "I mean, just so no one would ever guess that he was a runaway priest."

"You'll do no such thing," Mom said. "Now, I need your word, both of you, that we won't breathe a word of this to anyone."

I looked at Maxey.

"Maxey," Mom said. "Have you already told someone about Father being here?"

"Of course not!" she puffed. "You were only gone an hour. I was studying for my religion test the whole time."

My bad feeling with warts grew a pea-soup green alien head.

"All right, it's settled, then. This stays in the family for now. Just the three of us will know, and *no one* else. I don't know how long Father Avila—"

"Frank," Maxey corrected her.

"Right, I don't know how long Frank will be with us, but he'll be a welcome guest. It's such a privilege to have him. I want you both to get to know him."

"Is he going to help pay for groceries and shampoo and stuff?" I asked. "We're kind of poor," I reminded Mom. "And he ate three pieces of turkey bacon."

Maxey butted in. "We are *not* poor! You better not be telling your little friends we are, either."

"Aren't we poor, Mom?" I asked.

"Cupcake, don't worry about money. It will all work out."

Maxey bounced on the couch. "Mom! Can I have a slumber party now that he's here? You always said if there were two adults in the house, we could have one. Please, Mom? Pretty please?"

"Maxey, stop, will you? You're making my head spin. He hasn't even moved in yet."

"Well, if he has to stay with us, do you think he could fix the bathtub upstairs so we can use it, Mom?" I asked.

"Oh!" Maxey said. "Let's ask him if he can put some shelves up in our room. I need a place for my makeup mirror that's by an outlet."

Mom picked up her whistle off the coffee table, and Maxey and I stopped talking. We hate the whistle. It's the one thing we agree on.

"Okay, meeting over," Mom said. "I'll tell Frank that we'd love to have him. Girls, do you know how lucky we are to have a priest staying in our home? Just think about all the prayers that will be said under this roof," she said. "We could use a few extra." She put her arms around us and gave a squeeze. We melted into it.

We get a lot of *go-team* butt slaps from my mom but not as many hugs. When you get one, you want to savor it. Maxey told me that before Dad went to prison, Mom used to hug us all the time. But then, Maxey is always telling me about these great things that happened before I was born, or too young to remember. Just to get my goat.

One thing I did know for sure was that my mom was very busy with her team, her coaching job, and me and Maxey. She didn't have a lot of extra time for anyone else. Especially somebody who was having God problems. I wasn't going to let anybody, not even a priest, mess up things in my house. It had happened once before, when I was too little to have any say about it. It wasn't going to happen again.

Mom hurried off to call Frank on his cell phone to tell him she'd talked it over with us.

Maxey raised an eyebrow. "I bet I know what Frank's prayers are going to be about while he's here."

"That you stop flirting with him?"

Maxey knuckled me in the arm, then put her palms together and raised her eyes upward. "Dear God, please make Coach fall in love with me."

"You lied to Mom," I said, knuckling her back. "You told Phil all about him. Why didn't you just tell the truth? She wouldn't have been mad. You didn't know that having a priest over for breakfast had to be top-secret."

"I only lied as a favor to Frank, which makes it an *official* favor to God, too."

"Telling a lie can't be a favor, Maxey!"

"You are so dim! Don't you get it? If Mom knew that Phil knew, she wouldn't let Frank stay with us because she'd worry Phil would tell everyone. And if Frank couldn't stay here, he might have to live like a fugitive, sleeping in his car and shaving in public bathrooms. Now, I'm sorry if you are offended by my lie, but I couldn't in good conscience let that happen to a priest. You'll understand after you've had the religion and ethics class with Sister Emmanuel. Some lies are for the greater good. And that's a quote," she said, poking me in the chest.

"But how are you going to keep Phil quiet? Because if I go to school tomorrow and everyone is whispering about us hiding a priest—well, you'll know what the kids are going to think, Maxey!"

"What? That we're helping a man of God?"

"No! That we're running a safe house for bad guys! First Dad, and now Father Frank, who *says* he's having a spiritual crisis, but what if he's run off with the Sunday collection money or maybe even some fancy church art?"

"First off, Phil doesn't breathe without checking with me," Maxey said. "Don't even worry about that. Besides, I've got some serious dirt on her. She wouldn't dare. Secondly, I can tell just by looking into Frank's eyes that he's no crook. Don't sweat it, Ef. You worry too much! Now vacate. I need to use the phone, and I don't want that big ear of yours anywhere near me."

"Mom says you're not supposed to make fun of me," I reminded her, my face hot. I do have one ear bigger than the other. "And you better not do it in front of Frank. You aren't going to be able to hide your evil ways much longer."

"*Frank* will understand what I have to put up with."

"*Frank* will call ahead and make reservations for you at the Hotel Hades."

And with that, I spun around. For once, I got the last word.

"Big ear," she whispered.

Chapter 8

Frank wasn't back in the house fifteen minutes before Maxey had hijacked him and put him to work. Mom tried to stop her, but Frank laughed and said he'd be happy to help. I went out to our car to do my homework. And I needed to think about how I was going to keep Booger Boy from tormenting Aurora so she wouldn't want to leave.

It had suddenly gotten very noisy in my house. Frank had such a deep voice. And he laughed too much.

When I came back in later, I found Maxey sitting on the toilet, handing him tools, smacking her overglossed lips, and flinging back her hair.

She put on the sickening voice she uses with me when an adult is nearby. "There you are, Effie! Isn't this exciting?

Frank is fixing the tub. That handle has been broken forever. I can't wait to take a bath!"

"Hi, Effie!" he called under his armpit.

I ducked out the door, mumbling hello. Priests and nuns belonged in churches and convents, not in my house in their regular clothes. Even if he was fixing the tub, which I did miss.

I thundered down the stairs. Pretty Girl hissed and swiped at me when I walked by. She'd been in a giant foul mood since Grandpa had died. You could hardly blame her. She missed living in her old house. She and Grandpa liked to listen to old-fashioned music together and share ice cream from a bowl. And every afternoon, he'd put on this big red apron with strawberries on it and tie it around him under his armpits. He looked pretty silly in it, but it used to belong to my grandma, so it was very sentimental to him and Pretty Girl. Then Grandpa would pull out the special furry bath mat and put it on the kitchen table. He'd make kissing noises until Pretty Girl came in, and then he'd give her a long combing and sing to her. Pretty Girl loved it when he made her hair all nice and fluffy. She'd turn her head from side to side and lift her chin, making sure he didn't miss a single place.

Then one morning about a year ago, Grandpa didn't wake up, and everything in her life changed. She lost the person who loved her most in the world; she lost her house, her music, her ice cream. The worst part was that we made her come live with us. We were noisy, and when she needed to be combed, we had to take her to the groomer. She would hardly let us lay a hand on her.

I was beginning to feel the same way as Pretty Girl. Frank was going to change everything.

I plopped down at the kitchen table, and it took me a moment before I saw what Mom was doing at the kitchen sink. "You're washing a chicken!" I gasped.

She turned to look at me. "Last I heard it was still legal in Texas."

"Mom! We always have hamburgers on Sunday night at our Team Meeting. Plus," I said, hurrying over to the calendar on the fridge, "look! It's the last Sunday of the month, and that means *take-out* hamburgers."

"I know, cupcake. But Frank went out and bought this wonderful free-range chicken from the butcher. It's a treat. I don't want to hurt his feelings."

"Couldn't you fix him the beautiful chicken, and he can eat it in here while we have our hamburgers and our meeting? I'm sure he doesn't want to interrupt us."

Mom laid the chicken in a roasting pan and then washed her hands for a long time. "He's fixing your bathtub, you know." She turned to look at me.

"You're not inviting him to our Team Meeting, are you?" I asked. "You can't, Mom. We talk about girl things."

"It might be nice for him to see what family life is like, Ef. He didn't have brothers or sisters growing up."

"Do you really think he wants to hear Maxey's weekly report on how many girls at St. Dom's get to wear grown-up bras and she'll *die* if she has to keep wearing plain white ones?"

"Let's just see how tonight goes, huh? We've got a new player on our team, Ef, and we can't act like he's not on the court."

I dropped my head down on the table. "Exactly how many days will he be here, Mom?"

"As many as he needs. I owe him big-time. I probably would have flunked out of college if he hadn't helped me. He tutored me through all my math and sciences, and even pulled some of my shifts at the Donut Hole so I could get my papers done. He's very smart, and one of the hardest workers I've ever met."

"More than *seven* days, do you think?" I asked.

"Effie!" Mom said.

"Well, will he be gone by St. Patrick's Day?"

"Keep that up, young lady, and *you* might be gone by then," she said, flicking a dish towel at me. "Set the table, and get some gratitude, huh? It's an honor to have a priest in our home, and he's brought us a lovely dinner."

I pulled the plates out of the cupboard and set his down next to Mom's. When she wasn't looking, I slipped the Whamo Burger take-out menu under his plate.

Just helping my new "teammate" get a clue!

• • •

I kept my fingers crossed all through dinner that Frank might want to skip the Team Meeting so he could go pray or something, but he told Mom he'd love to join us. I kept my eyes on my plate and gave my free-range chicken leg a dirty look. If I had to eat it, I hoped it at least would pouf out my boobs a little bit.

At one minute before seven o'clock, Maxey came floating down the staircase wearing a shiny, slinky robe like the models in the Victoria's Secret catalogs. And she was wearing matching eye shadow. Mom chased her back upstairs.

I picked up a magazine and hid behind it while they were gone.

Frank was quiet for a moment, but I could feel him staring at me. I scooched farther behind the magazine.

"Your mom is very proud of what good grades you get in school, Effie," he said.

"Thank you," I mumbled.

"What's your favorite subject right now?" he asked.

"Reading," I said, hoping he'd get the hint.

"I love to read," he said. "Do you have a favorite author?"

"No."

"Do you like sports?"

"No."

"Not even basketball? Your mom is a sensational player and coach."

"No. Yes."

He paused. Like he wasn't sure if he should keep trying. Then, "I didn't see you too much today. Did you have a lot of homework?"

I sighed. "I'm working on something very secret and I can't really discuss it."

"Oh, I see. Me too."

I lowered the magazine. "You are?"

"Yep."

"You're working on something very secret?"

He nodded.

I stared at him. But now he was studying all the books on the coffee table. I knew it! There was something not right about this guy.

"I guess if you *wanted* to, you could tell me about it," I said.

"Well, it's top-secret, so I can't talk about it."

"Oh, right," I said. I'd have to be very careful if I wanted to catch him in a lie.

"So is that your car out front, or did you, you know, 'borrow' it?" I whispered.

Chapter 9

"Mine," he whispered back.

"Priests have their own cars?"

He nodded. "Most of them do."

"Where'd you get the money?"

He looked around the room and then leaned in. My heart began to pump hard.

"My Uncle Ruben left me some money."

"Uh-oh," I said, shaking my head. I licked my finger to turn a page of my magazine. Cool as I could be.

"Uh-oh, what?"

"You were supposed to turn that money in to the church! Because there was this nun at the Old Sisters' Home in Tyler Wash that won a million dollars in the lottery, and she had to give *all* the money to the Vatican in Rome."

"Really!" He looked shocked.

"Yup!" I said. "So you better watch out in case you have any leftover money from your uncle."

"Thanks for the tip."

"Our VW bug is really old and farts out black smoke, and the heater doesn't work. Mom says it doesn't seem right to get a new car when so many people in Tyler Wash lost money to my dad. She thinks if we get a new one, people will come knocking on our door asking for their money back. Maybe you should park yours around the block so people don't think we're throwing *our* money away on fancy cars."

Mom and Maxey came down the stairs at that moment. Maxey was dressed in her regular Team Meeting sweats and her face was scrubbed and red. Her hair was pulled back tight in a ponytail. She looked mad and mortified. Mom had that exasperated look she got when one of her players made a stupid foul.

"Here we are!" Mom said.

Maxey flounced herself into a chair, ripped out the ponytail, and began to pick at her split ends.

Mom cleared her throat in Maxey's direction.

"Sorry to keep you all waiting," Maxey said.

"Not at all!" Frank said. "Effie and I were having a nice chat."

"Great!" Mom said. "Well, why don't we get started? Frank, would you like to start us with a prayer?"

Maxey and I looked at her wild-eyed. We didn't pray at the Team Meeting!

He hesitated. Looked around at us.

Now, this was suspicious. All the priests I'd ever met

couldn't wait to pray. Most of the time you couldn't get them to stop.

"Do you usually say a prayer before this meeting?"

Mom shook her head. "No, but it would be a very nice thing to start."

"Well, how about instead of a formal prayer, we just each say something about this week we feel grateful for."

Maybe he didn't know any prayers! Maybe he wasn't even a priest at all!

"I'll start," Maxey said, getting her second wind. "I'm very grateful that you've come to live with us, Frank. And I hope you're here long enough to help Mom throw me a slumber party, for which I'd be very grateful. Amen."

"Effie?" Mom asked.

"Um," I said, trying to think fast. "Well, I'm grateful that we don't have a lot of money because you can't thread a needle with a camel and I do want to go to heaven some-day." Everyone looked puzzled by that, so I added, "Sister said that rich people can't go to heaven. Just like camels can't get through the eye of a needle, so don't even try." I gave Frank a stern look. "And, I'm grateful for my two best friends, and that our grandpa looks after our family from heaven, and that there's a cop that lives down the street. Amen."

Mom said she was grateful that Frank was here and how lucky we were.

Frank flashed his white teeth at each of us. "I'm grateful that you've welcomed me into your home."

Not for long, buster, I thought. If he was a priest, he was the world's worst ever. Maybe he got kicked out! For forgetting his prayers. And for not turning in his money from Uncle Ruben. He could have made up that whole story about being promoted to a bishop. Probably figured Mom for a sucker, after what Dad got past her.

Mom picked up her clipboard. During the week, she'd jot down things that she wanted us to talk about, and if we thought of something, we'd tell her and she'd add it to her list.

"Let's see . . . I've got two late practices this week, on Tuesday and Thursday. Girls, I'll need you to start dinner. Maxey, you take Tuesday, and Effie, you'll do Thursday." Mom looked over at Maxey, ready for her usual argument about having to eat anything I cooked, but Maxey didn't say a word.

"Kath, I can help with that, too," Frank said.

Kath? It had been so long since I'd heard anyone call Mom anything but "Coach," I almost forgot her name was Katherine. I did not like him calling her "Kath" one bit.

"Oh, and Effie, you wanted to talk about some bathroom-sharing issues. Is there a problem?" Mom asked.

I glanced at Maxey, who threw me a frantic look. She knew I was planning on complaining about how she kept leaving big mouth prints on the mirror. She liked to see how she looked close up when she was kissing. But I couldn't say that in front of Frank. It would do her in.

"Nothing," I said. "We worked it out."

Maxey closed her eyes a second in relief and then said, "I don't have any issues, either, Mom."

"Nothing?" Mom was incredulous. This was a Maloney family first.

We both lifted our shoulders and dropped them at the very same second. Like we'd practiced all day.

"Well, now I'm doubly grateful you're here, Frank." She smiled at him. "How about you? Anything you'd like to tell us or ask us?"

"I noticed that you're having some trouble out back with a gopher, or maybe a whole pack of them. And it looks like you could use some gardening help. Your yard has great potential! You've got some amazing trees. I wondered if you would mind if I tried to fix it up a bit? Make it a nice spot for all of you to enjoy."

Mom sighed. "Oh, Frank, I'd love it. It's all I can do on the weekends to mow the front yard. We've had to just let the backyard go, I'm afraid. I really wouldn't know where to get started."

"We tried to get the gopher," Maxey said. "But he's too happy back there."

Frank laughed. "Well, I'd like to give it a try. Okay with all of you?"

"Sure!" Mom said. "It's all yours."

"Mom? The slumber party?" Maxey said. "Can we talk about that? Please? Please? Before he leaves? I'm almost the only girl in my class that hasn't had one. It's embarrassing."

Mom pinched the bridge of her nose like she did whenever the slumber party issue came up. She believed that everybody needed at least eight hours of sleep a night. The idea of staying awake with a bunch of girls all night sounded like pure torture to her. At least, that's what I heard her tell Mrs. Korn on the phone when I was sort of eavesdropping pressed against her office door.

"Tell you, what, Max. You pull that religion grade up to an A, and you've got a deal."

Maxey's face started to grow pink, and she balled up her fists. But she stopped one nanosecond before she blew.

She smiled. It was her innocent look that really should come with a flashing red Danger sign. "Frank, maybe you could tutor me?"

Chapter 10

On Tuesday morning, I had my face pressed to the greasy window of the school bus as we pulled into St. Dom's. Nit's face was right next to mine.

"Do you see her yet?" she asked.

Aurora's usually easy to spot. She's tall, and the only kid who carries a basketball wherever she goes. We'd told her to wait for us so we could all walk to class together. We wanted to give her moral support since everyone knew she'd been suspended the day before. Nit and I were worried that she'd get teased and maybe get so mad she'd do something to get suspended again.

"Where is she?" I said. "C'mon, let's go," I said. "Maybe she forgot and went to class."

We jammed into the aisle of kids waiting to get off. Everybody seemed to have the slows.

"Hey, Marcus!" I heard a kid near the back yell. "Let us know if you need some protection today from that big fourth-grade kid. Hear she's back today!"

All the kids laughed, and I didn't feel one bit sorry for him. He deserved it and more for all the misery he'd caused her.

I jumped the last three steps down, Nit on my heels.

"You wait here," I said, "in case she comes. I'll go check the classroom."

"Okay!"

I dodged past all the kids with their enormous backpacks, weaving in and out like a running back. I arrived at the door of my classroom and burst in.

Oh, no! Aurora's seat was empty.

"Good-morning-Mr.-Giles-have-you-seen-Aurora-Triboni-yet?" I asked, panting.

"Good morning to you, Miss Maloney," he said, peering over the top of his glasses. "I have not," he said, and then lifted a sheet next to his books. "But I see that she is on my Absent list for today."

"That was just for yesterday. She is definitely here today."

"No, this is today's list. We are not expecting Miss Triboni."

What did that mean?

The bell rang, and Nit came skidding up to the door. Her eyes grew wide when she saw Aurora's empty chair.

"Take your seats, please!" Mr. Giles said.

"She's in the principal's office," Kayla said as she sashayed past me. "With both her parents," she added, smug.

• • •

The minutes, then hours on our classroom clock ticked by, but Aurora never showed up. Nit and I started sending each other frantic looks and urgent folded-up messages.

Me: What is taking SO LONG?? Do you think she's okay?
Nit: *Sister or Aurora?:—/*
Me:: Aurora! It's almost lunchtime! We've got to go help her.
Nit: *How??*
Me: Do something really bad so Mr. Giles will send us both to see Sister.
Nit: *He'd never believe it. We're pretty good kids, Ef.*

I was scribbling down my ideas about that when a pair of very long men's shoes appeared next to my desk.

I gulped and looked up.

"Miss Maloney? I see you've started your English lesson early and are writing an essay of some sort. Perhaps you'll read it to class?"

Even though I was trying to figure out how to get in trouble, now that I was, I got scared. "Um, no thanks, Mr. Giles. I mean, you don't really want me to read it."

"Actually, I do," he said, folding his arms across his chest. "I'm all ears."

"Wull, maybe we could skip that part and I could just go straight to the principal's office and get in a little bit of trouble for not paying attention."

"I better go too," Nit chimed in. "I haven't been paying attention either."

Donal slapped his forehead. "Janey Mack! Nah you've done it."

"Miss Maloney?" he said, motioning me to the front.

I slunk up the row with my wrinkly paper, then turned to the class.

"Nice and loud, please," he said.

I cleared my throat. "I bet it would make Mr. Giles really mad if I went over and erased his dumb old drawing of the canal. Or maybe I could empty the trash can over Kayla's head—" I broke off when I heard her gasp. "I was just kidding around, sir."

"I think we've heard enough," he said. He reached into his desk and pulled out his green pad. Everyone knew what that was.

A ticket to the principal's office.

Chapter 11

I thrust my green slip at Dottie, the principal's assistant, who raised an eyebrow as she read it. "Well, this is a first, Effie."

"I know." I looked at the candy dish on her desk. My mouth was dry as dust. But I was pretty sure the candy wasn't meant for kids who were in trouble.

Principal Obermeyer had a whole drawer full of chocolate in her office, and when I came to visit her, she always gave me some. We both loved dark chocolate. After she saved me from being hit by lightning a few weeks back, she told me I could come talk to her anytime. I sure needed to talk to her today. I wish she'd get back from her sabbatical.

"Take a seat," Dottie said, pointing to the bench, where Sleepy William was curled up. He was a fifth grader who got sent to the principal's office nearly every day for sleeping in class.

Dottie buzzed Sister on the intercom and told her I was there.

"Go on in, honey." She nodded at the big brown door.

"Is Aurora Triboni in there with her?" I whispered.

She just pressed her lips together and shooed me along.

I took a breath and headed in.

• • •

Sister Emmanuel didn't look right sitting behind Principal Obermeyer's desk. Her giant black dog, Bear, lay next to her. He raised his head when I walked in but did not wag his tail. He was busy chewing the edge of the rug, getting dog spit on it. Bear had a terrible slobber problem and was famous for his smoky, deadly farts.

I looked around the room to see if Aurora was hanging from the coat tree, or maybe gagged and bound in the corner.

Nope.

Sister didn't invite me to sit down or offer me a beverage like Principal Obermeyer did. She read the green sheet a very long time. Maybe she was one of those slow readers. Bear growled as he wrestled with the rug fringe.

"How do you like being the substitute principal?" I asked, trying to make polite conversation.

She looked up at me without expression. "Park yourself, young lady."

"Yes, ma'am." I smoothed my skirt over my knees, trying to keep them still.

"I don't like it when students interrupt teachers who are trying to give their lessons. Mr. Giles works particularly hard on his."

"Yes, he does," I said. "I'm very sorry."

"What exactly are you sorry about, Miss Maloney?"

"That I interrupted him?"

"Anything else?"

"Oh—what I said about Kayla Quintana. I wouldn't really empty the trash on her head. My mother would skin me alive if I did that."

"Good for her," she said. "Anything else?"

"Anything else that I'm sorry about?" I asked, licking my lips.

She sighed and nodded.

"Um . . . well, I heard you were visiting with the Tribonis this morning. I'm sorry that I missed seeing them. Are they still around, by any chance?"

Sister came around the front of her desk then and perched on the edge. Her boots dangled in front of me. "Are you being fresh, young lady?"

"No, Sister. I'm just worried about Aurora."

"That's not your job."

"Yes, it is, Sister!" I blurted. "She's my best friend and I'd do anything for her. You didn't suspend her again, did you?"

"Miss Triboni decided on her own that she wanted to go home. She has some thinking to do. So do her parents."

"But—but, Sister! We have a test on Friday. She'll get behind."

"Her mother will pick up her assignments each day."

I shook my head back and forth. "No! Make her come here, please, Sister. If you're not careful, she won't come back ever! She wants to play sports and her dad is trying to get her a college scholarship, but she's only in fourth grade—"

Sister put up her hand in warning. "That is entirely enough!"

A terrible, hot, rotten smell came toward us.

"Bear!" Sister barked. She went over and threw the window open. Too late.

I tried to hold my breath.

"That was most ungentlemanly of you, Bear." Sister clicked her tongue.

"May I go, Sister?" I choked. I didn't know if it was the fart or the idea that Aurora wasn't going to be at school for a while that was making my eyes burn.

"You and I aren't quite finished here. I believe school detention is a total waste of time, but I do believe in community service as a teaching tool. I don't want to ever see you in this office again, Miss Maloney. Your poor mother has enough on her hands without you becoming a behavior problem at school."

"Yes, Sister."

She handed me a tissue.

"You may walk Bear for me on Friday afternoons until Principal Obermeyer returns. I have a standing engagment, and Bear needs his exercise. I will discuss this with your mother to make sure that it won't inconvenience her."

I nodded, only half listening. My mind was trying to absorb the terrible news about Aurora.

"Secondly, you will visit Sister Josephine in the hospital and read to her once a week until she is returned to us."

"Yes, ma'am. Anything else?"

"Mr. Giles is fond of shortbread. If I were you, I'd bake him some."

Chapter 12

Nit and I were hoping we could take a quick trip over to Aurora's house right after school, but Mom was waiting for me at the curb when school let out. Sister or Dottie must have called her. I was in for it now.

She was standing outside our old VW bug talking to Maxey, who looked as happy as if Christmas had arrived in February.

Maxey lunged at me the minute she saw me. "It's all over school that you got sent to the principal's office today. And that you threatened Kayla Quintana. You are in *so* much trouble," she said, grinning. "Plus, I've just been filling Mom in about what Aurora did last Friday. You never told her!"

"Maxey, get on the bus," Mom said. She gave me a once-over, like she was making sure I was still me and not some alien.

"The bus?" Maxey whined. "Why take the bus if you're right here?"

"I need to speak to your sister. Privately. I'll see you at home. Don't forget you're starting dinner tonight. Effeline, get in the car."

I was in for it.

Mom didn't say anything until we were a few blocks away from school. I tried asking her if she had a nice day, but she gave me a glare over the top of her sunglasses.

Finally, the dam broke. "Sister Emmanuel called me and told me what you did today. I left work. Do you know what that means?"

I scraped my lip with my teeth. "Do they cut your pay?"

She sighed and pulled off her glasses. Planted them on the top of her head. "No, but I had to send my team to study hall, and we wasted an entire practice. And believe me, those girls need the practice!"

"I'm really sorry, Mom," I said, feeling pretty terrible. I was so worried about finding Aurora that I didn't think about all the trouble I might make.

"Effie, what *happened*?"

"It's a very long story," I said. "You probably need to get back to work. I could tell you later."

"Yes, I do," she said. "And you're going with me, young lady."

I knew what was coming. Dirty Towel Duty in the gym.

"Let's hear it, Effie. You are not getting out of this car until I hear the whole story. All of it!"

I didn't really know where to start. Things had gone from bad to worse so fast. I took a big breath and plunged in.

"It all started because of the singing valentine that Booger Boy sent to Aurora in the middle of class."

"Please don't call him that."

"Sorry. Marcus has a terrible crush on Aurora, and he made her so mad that she called him a bad name and drug him around the parking lot, and since Principal Obermeyer is gone Sister Emmanuel is in charge and she suspended her for a day and said Aurora couldn't go to Angel Scout camp!"

"Slow down, Effie! You're giving me the spins."

"Okay, but Aurora was supposed to come back to school today but then she didn't because she was on the Absent list and then Kayla told me she was in Sister Emmanuel's office with her parents—"

"Who? Kayla or Aurora?" Mom interrupted.

"Aurora. So I figured she'd be a little late to class, but then she never came and me and Nit got worried and started sending notes about it and decided we needed to get into trouble so we could go to Sister's office and find out WHAT was going on—"

"Effie! Stop!" Mom said. "Take a breath!"

I sucked up a deep one. "I was writing this note to Nit about some ideas I had for getting us in trouble and then Mr. Giles came up and caught me and made me read it in front of the whole class, and then he sent just me to see Sister Emmanuel even though Nit wanted to go too but Aurora wasn't there and Sister said she'd gone home with her parents and they all needed to do some thinking about whether she would come back."

"*Slooower!*" Mom said, pulling into the high school lot.

"I'm so worried she won't come back because maybe deep

in her heart Aurora wants to go to public school because maybe there are other girls there with breasts so the boys don't stare as much and the teachers are better coaches so she can learn sports—Mom, do you think you could coach Aurora in basketball and then maybe she'll want to stay at St. Dominic's?"

Mom pulled into her special teacher's parking slot and yanked hard on the brake. She popped off her seat belt and turned to look at me.

"First off, all I care about right now is what you did, not what Aurora or Nit or Sister Emmanuel did. Got that?"

"Yes, ma'am."

"I'm very unhappy about what you did. You embarrassed yourself and our family. The last thing I need is the Quintana family giving me grief that you've threatened their daughter. Even your sister would know better than to pull something like that," she said.

This was a new all-time low for me. Mom thought Maxey's behavior was better than mine!

"Our family already carries a big burden in this town. People aren't going to give us any breaks."

"I know, Mom."

"Sister told me about her having you walk Bear and visiting Sister Josephine. Does that seem fair to you?"

"I guess . . ."

"Do you think you deserve to be grounded at home, too?" Mom raised an eyebrow at me.

"Well . . . okay, but could you start it after I go to Aurora's, Mom? I really need to talk to her. I just know I can convince her to come back."

"Effie!" Mom said. "You are not Aurora's keeper. It's up to her and her family to figure out what is right for her."

"But they're worried about getting her into a good college! She's only in fourth grade. She needs her best friends."

She pulled her keys out of the ignition and dropped them into her bag. "This has to be her decision. Got it?"

I nodded. But Mom didn't understand about Aurora and how sensitive she was about boys paying too much attention to her.

"Let's go, toots. Bring your backpack. You can sit in my office and do your homework until it's time to go home."

"Aren't I going to do the towels?"

"Nope—I've got something else in mind for you at home."

"Can I call Aurora real quick before I start? I mean, just to make sure she's okay and not to try to convince her of anything?"

"Effie, do you hear what I'm saying? This is Aurora's problem, not yours! I want you to focus on Effie. And to help you do that, I'm grounding you from Aurora until next Sunday—no visits, no calls, no e-mail!"

"But, Mom!"

She put up her penalty finger.

This was the worst punishment ever—grounded from one of my best friends!

"Being loyal to your friends is admirable, Effie. But you went way too far this time, and I want you to learn from this. You crossed the line today."

I opened the car door. The hinges screeched. I felt like doing the same thing, but it wouldn't help.

"Effie, why didn't you tell me that Aurora had been suspended from school?"

I shrugged. "I dunno." I almost said because every time I tried to get a word in edgewise, Frank was hogging you.

Luckily, I kept my mouth shut.

Chapter 13

I didn't think it was possible to have a punishment that even came close to being as unfair as being grounded from Aurora for nearly a whole week. But after dinner that night, Mom announced that I was going to be Frank's backyard helper all day on Sunday.

That bad news came after she gave Maxey and me a very long talk about how we had to get along in school—even better than the other kids. Dad had used up all the trouble points one family could have, I guess. One more helping of unfairness on our plates. Was this ever going to end?

Since Maxey wasn't in trouble, but I was, she sat there nearly humming with happiness through the whole thing. Her eyes went dark when she realized that I would be with

Frank all day Sunday, but it passed. The idea of my being punished was just too good.

I was hoping that I might even come down with some horrible disease by then—something very contagious that Frank would be so worried about catching, he would pack up his car and leave. Because I was getting the funny feeling he wasn't planning on leaving anytime soon. Even though I very helpfully pulled out the Apartments for Rent section of the paper and left it near his place at the table. He glanced at it, and then found the sports section instead. Why would a priest read the sports pages anyway? He should have been reading the section that listed all the people who had died. Then he could have said some prayers for them and called their families to see if they needed him to do their funerals. I had an awful lot of clues about Father Frank Avila that were just not adding up!

I excused myself after dinner and went up to use the phone. I had to ask Nit to call Aurora for me right away.

Maxey followed me upstairs like she knew I was about to do something secret. We had one of those old-fashioned phones in our upstairs hallway that was attached to the wall, so it was hard to get much privacy. But Maxey had stretched the cord on the handset way out from making a lot of illegal calls to boys after lights-out. She'd pull the phone way into our closet and close the doors so I couldn't hear. Supposedly. I kept telling her she was going to electrocute herself, but so far no luck on that.

It was my turn to climb into the closet phone booth. Maxey watched me from the bed; then she picked up her big old religion book and started reading. Like I was going to fall for that.

Nit's sister, Phil, picked up after the second ring. "Hi, Phil," I said. "It's Effie. Can I talk to Nit, please?"

"No."

"C'mon, Philomena, please. It's an emergency."

"Nope. She's grounded from you."

"Whaat?" I gasped.

"You heard me."

"Wull, when did this happen?"

"*Wull,* today!" she said, making fun of me.

"Are you sure she's grounded from *me?* I mean, is she just regular grounded so she can't talk to anyone, *including* me?"

"No, just you. I told Mother that you two were writing terrible notes to each other in class today and your teacher was very upset. She can talk to anyone else she likes."

"Can she talk to Aurora?"

"Yep."

This was just too weird. In my whole life, I'd never heard of this punishment where the mother grounds the kid from their best friend, but now it was all over town. Like an epidemic!

I thought fast. "Okay, since Nit can't talk to me, but she can talk to Aurora, could you give her a message to give to Aurora from me?"

"Are you kidding?" She laughed in a way that wasn't friendly. "Do you think I'm like your personal assistant or something?"

"Please, Phil, it's really important!"

"No way. This is your mess, not mine." She hung up with a click.

I threw open the closet doors, half expecting Maxey to fall in where she'd been listening on the other side. But she was still lying on the bed with her nose in her book.

"Maxey! You gotta help me."

"I'm studying. Hey, did you know that St. Therese, the Little Flower, was only fifteen when she became a nun? She got special permission from the Pope. If Frank becomes a bishop, I bet he could get me in," she said, smug.

"Great, that's so interesting. But I need you to help me."

She turned the page. "With what?"

"I need you to call Phil and get her to give a message to Nit from me to give to Aurora."

"You're grounded from Aurora," she said.

"I know! But I'm just not supposed to be talking to her. This isn't talking to her. It's talking to you."

"Hmm," she said. "It still feels like it's wrong."

"It's a tiny bit wrong, but for a very right reason. Maxey, please?"

"Oh, all right."

"You will?" I said, surprised.

"I just said I would, didn't I?"

"I know, but what do I have to do for you? What's the catch?"

She shrugged. "No trade. Can't a big sister do a favor for her little sister out of family love? St. Therese and her sister loved each other so much they joined the same convent so that they could be together always."

"Okay, great!" I handed her the phone. "I'll dial."

"What's the message?"

"Tell Phil to tell Nit to call Aurora right away and tell her to come back to school! That Nit and I will make sure nobody teases her and we'll work on getting her into a good college. And, well, tell Nit and Aurora that I'm going to write them a letter tonight. Mom won't even let me use e-mail! And they should write me back—but with a letter, not an e-mail."

"Why are you writing Nit a letter?" Maxey asked. "You'll see her at school tomorrow."

"It's the same letter for both of them. I want them to read it and write me back. Just do it, okay, Maxey? Please?"

Maxey punched in the numbers. "Phil, it's me. I want you to give a message to your sister from Effie."

She twirled the cord around her finger while she listened to Phil, who apparently was giving her some grief about it.

"Just do it." She paused and took a big breath and listened some more. Then she covered the mouthpiece. "Don't worry, she'll come around. She's just saving face."

"Okay, then go get some paper, Phil, to write it down. You'll never remember the whole thing. I don't want you to screw it up."

Maxey handed me the phone. "Done, she'll take the message now." She turned back to her religion book like she couldn't wait to finish what she was reading. Did it include a section called "Ten Tips to Get Boys to Suck Face with You"? I couldn't imagine why she was so glued to it all.

I heard Phil come back on the line with a big annoyed sigh. "All right," she said. "Shoot."

Tuesday night, Feb 26

Dear Nit and Aurora,

I can't ~~beleive~~ believe (See, Nit? I am working on my spelling!) that our mothers all grounded us from each other. My mom won't even let me e-mail you!

Aurora, we waited for you this morning and then when Kayla told

74

us you were in Sister's office we tried to get to you but everything backfired and I ended up getting in big trouble with Mr. Giles. I thought we had it all worked out so you would stay with us at St. Dom's. You are coming back, right???

The three of us have to stick together! I used to be so lonely—we all were. Nit, you hardly even ever talked. I'm sorry that I wasn't nicer to you back then. Now I know that you felt bad inside just like I did. I'm sorry, Nit.

You had Kayla, Aurora, but she was a terrible friend. I remember you told me that the first time you went to spend the night at Kayla's house she ignored you the whole time. You said that she didn't really like you after all, she just liked telling people that you spent the night at her house.

Mom is punishing me for today by making me work in the yard on Sunday, but after that, can you both meet at Big Arlene's in the afternoon? I'm already dying to see you.

Your friend for eternity,
Effie XO

February 27, 5:26 a.m.

Dear Effie and Aurora,

I can hardly sleep trying to figure out what we are going to do! My mom is kind of freaked about me being friends with you two because of everything that happened at school. Phil made it sound a lot worse than it really was.

Aurora, I'm going to miss you a lot this week. I hope-hope-hope you are coming back next week? But if you decide not to, I still want to be your friend. 4-ever! You are such a cool girl.

Effie, at least I get to see you at school today! I'm sorry that everything turned out so horrible for you. It wasn't fair. I should have gotten in trouble, too. I'm going to do your punishments with you, okay?

Before the two of you were my best friends, I hated going to school so much. Now I can't wait to go every day. I feel so lucky!

Friends forever!
Trinity Finch, "Nit"

Wednesday, February 27, 2007

Dear Effie and Nit,

I have to write this real quick while my mom is taking a shower. I'm supposed to be working on math. Sorry I wasn't home when you called last night, Nit. I went over to Sam Houston's to watch the sixth-grade girls play ball. They have a great team!

You're probably wondering why I'm not at school with the two of you. Remember when we saw Chip with the Turner boys? They all went to town that day and got arrested for stealing chew. My parents are freaking out and Dad wants to send him away to a military school to straighten him out, and it's expensive. Me going to public school now could save money.

Uh-oh, better go. I hear the shower turning off. So, right now, me, Dad, and Mom are taking the week to think it over. I'll keep you posted. I'm grounded this week, but let's try to get together this weekend, okay? I really miss U both!

Hugs,
Aurora

Chapter 14

It took about three whole weeks for Sunday to arrive. At least, it felt that way! I was so excited to see my best friends I could hardly sleep the night before.

I got up early and put on my crummiest clothes to help Frank in the yard. I couldn't wait to get started and get done so I could go meet Aurora and Nit at Big Arlene's.

But when I went downstairs, Mom sent me marching right back up to put on a nice outfit for church. We hadn't gone the night before since I'd been over at the hospital reading the Bible to Sister Josephine. She looked like she was dead, but the nurse kept promising me she wasn't.

"Frank is already outside now," I argued. "Aren't you going to make him go to Mass?"

"I invited him and he is choosing to visit with God in the

backyard today. Now go change and get the lead out, young lady," she said.

"Why can't I just visit with Backyard God?" I said. "Besides, don't you think doing yard work with a priest is as good as being at church?"

"Now, miss!" She pointed up the stairs.

I clomped back up, letting her know with each step how much I disagreed with her. It wasn't that I minded going to church so much, especially on Free Doughnut Sunday. But if I had to go to Mass and then do yard work, it could take all day.

When I got up to our room, Maxey was kneeling next to the bed with her head down and her eyes closed.

"You got something in your eye?"

She didn't answer.

"Lose something under the bed?"

She made the sign of the cross, then turned. "I was saying my prayers."

I looked around to see if Mom or Frank or maybe even Jesus was in the room. "What for? You're going to church in about five minutes!"

"Frank says talking to God first thing in the morning is an essential part of one's spiritual development."

"But what's that got to do with you? You always say that God already knows what you want, so you shouldn't have to beg for it every day."

"Frank is very interested in my soul."

"Yeah, right," I said, pulling off my sneakers and hurling them into the closet.

"You are such an ungrateful brat, Effie!"

"What am I supposed to be grateful about? That he's here hiding and mooching off of us?"

She grabbed my arm. "Don't you dare talk about him like that!"

I yanked it back. "So now you're going to be in love with him? Mr. Constantino will be heartbroken." He was her science teacher, and Maxey had been crazy about him all year long.

"If you do anything that upsets Frank, I swear I will kill you, Effie."

I turned away and pulled my tee over my head, then fished my denim skirt out of the dirty-laundry basket, along with a pair of socks that didn't look too grungy. I did a quick sniff test. I grabbed my Tinker Bell spray cologne and gave them a few good pumps.

"You are completely disgusting," Maxey said. "I'm not going to sit in the same pew with you."

"Great! Now I know what I'll be giving thanks for."

· · ·

By the time we got back from Mass and free doughnuts, our backyard was a bigger mess than ever. The gopher holes were huge now, and there were mountains of dirt and cut-up bushes stacked everywhere.

Frank had marked off a giant area with little stakes and string. Like maybe he was putting in a swimming pool, which I hoped he was. But then I cancelled the wish because it would take too long. And the longer he was here, the better the chance that Mom might decide she really needed a man in her life. Even she looked a little scared when she went with me out back.

If Frank had littler ears and two buck teeth, we might have thought he was the backyard gopher. He was filthy dirty. But he looked very happy with himself. He put down his shovel and came over, lifting up his T-shirt to wipe his face. I gasped and looked away. I did not want to see a priest's belly button, especially on a Sunday. "You've been busy! Is all this dirt ours, or did you order it?" Mom looked at all the piles.

He laughed. "All yours, ma'am. And this is perfect timing. I'll be very glad to have a helper!"

Mom nudged me from behind, and I bared my teeth in my fake smile-on-demand.

"What happened to our grass?" I asked.

"Well, it was more like crabgrass. I'm taking it out for the labyrinth."

"What's a labyrinth?" I asked.

"Remember when I went to that coaches' conference last year in Arizona?" Mom asked. "The place where we stayed had this gorgeous garden with a labyrinth in it. It's like a maze."

"Yeah, I have a book of mazes," I said. "It's like a puzzle. You try to find your way through it without getting to a dead end."

"Right!" Mom said. "This kind of labyrinth is on the ground, and you walk it."

"Oh," I said. "Is it like a race and you try to beat the other players?"

Frank laughed. "No, it's not a race, but there could be other people walking it with you."

"Are you allowed to talk to the other players?" I asked. "Maybe give them hints if they get stuck?"

"People usually don't talk in it, Ef. It's a quiet, private thing."

"Oh." This sounded about as exciting as watching potatoes grow.

"Anyway, you know how I'm always going on about my dream backyard? Well, I showed Frank this picture of one I'm in love with, and he says he can give our yard a makeover. Plus, he says there will be room to put in a labyrinth for us! Can you believe it?"

Frank wiped some sweat off his forehead. "This would be an ideal place for a labyrinth. You've got these beautiful trees all around, and it's really peaceful out here. The one I'm going to build will be made out of big flat stones." He motioned to the area right in front of us. "This will be the mouth of it, and then it heads off here—" He pointed to the right. "I'll plant grass all around it. This is going to be such a great space for all of you."

"But what's it for?" I asked.

Mom poked me in the side to let me know she didn't like my snotty tone.

Frank got all dreamy looking. "That's the beautiful mystery of a labyrinth. It just *is*. You'll bring purpose to it. Labyrinths are great to use if you have a problem, or something you can't quite work out. You start walking the path thinking about the problem, or praying, and sometimes when you're done, you have an answer."

"What about the gopher?" I asked. "He'll just dig everything up."

"I'm working on that," he said. "I've poured ammonia down his tunnels. It won't hurt him, but he won't like it. And I'm going to plant some caper spurge. Gophers hate the smell of its seeds and roots. I suspect your gopher is going to be sending out a change-of-address form to his friends very soon."

"Thank the gods," Mom said. "I was about ready to call in the Texas Rangers to help me. Well . . . I'm going to leave the two of you to get at it." She went over and gave Frank a slap on the shoulder as in "Go, Team." "Have fun, you two!" Swatted me, too.

I shoved my hands in my pockets. "Where do I start?" I said. "And, 'scuse me, but how long do you think this will take?"

He picked up his shovel again. "Are you in a big hurry?"

"I have a very important meeting with my best friends today. An *emergency*."

"Fair enough," he said. He looked at his watch. "It's eleven o'clock now. How about we work until two, including lunch, and then I'll cut you loose."

Three whole hours! "Okay."

"Come sit with me a minute, Effie," he said, motioning to the last patch of crabgrass he hadn't pulled out.

"Did our explanation about what a labyrinth is for make sense?"

I shrugged. "You don't hop in it, do you?" I was trying to picture it.

He chuckled. "Well, you could, but most people just walk slowly. Sometimes they stand in one place for a while. And I don't think it has to be just for grown-ups. I'm hoping this will be a tool for you and Maxey to use."

Stash some cute boys out here and Maxey might use it.

"You and Maxey inherited a lot of grown-up problems—the kind most kids don't have to deal with. I want you to have a private, peaceful place where you can come think and sort some of that out." He looked around. "I'm going to put a couple of benches out here too, for just sitting, maybe reading, and a beautiful fountain."

"How long is this going to take you?" He made Mom really happy, but that was the good part and the bad part. I didn't want her getting too used to him being around.

"The thing about walking a labyrinth," he said, "and about making them, I think, is that it should be about the doing, not so much about the getting it done. Does that make sense?"

"Is this a trick question, Father—I mean, Frank?"

"Not really, but I'd like for us to think about doing this work in a different way than we might normally."

"Does it mean that you're not allowed to think about how long it might take?" I asked.

"Yeah, it's more about the doing. Can you think of something that you like doing even more than you like getting it done?"

Mom did not warn me there was going to be a pop quiz on the yard work first. Geez. I thought hard. "I like eating cookie dough before it gets turned into cookies. Is that what you mean?"

"Yeah," he said, nodding. "So let's think of our work today as being the cookie dough, and right now we're not going to think about how the cookies are going to turn out. We're enjoying the dough today, and that's all that matters."

"Yes, sir." Two sermons already and it wasn't even noon.

"Just call me Frank, Effie," he said. "I'd like us to be friends."

"How come you don't go to church like most priests?" I blurted. "Father McCabe goes every day."

"That's a good question." He stood up and handed me a small hand shovel. "Here, you can help me pull out the rest of this crabgrass."

He started digging. I waited for him to answer, but he was quiet for a long time. I sighed and started hacking away at the grass. Whenever you really want a grown-up to answer a question, they won't. Normally, you can't get them to stop answering questions, even when you don't want to hear it.

Finally, when I'd given up that he'd ever speak again, he said in a firm kind of voice, "I'm sorting some things out about the church right now, Ef. But not about God— I'm clear on that. And, as I'm sure you know, He or She is everywhere."

The back door banged just then, and Maxey came out carrying iced tea on a tray like she was a fancy waitress. She was still wearing her dress from church even though she'd been home a long time now.

"Here you go, Frank!" she said, putting down the tray on an old stump. She grabbed the glass of iced tea and handed it to him. It was one of our best glasses, and she'd put lemon slices in it. And she'd made her disgusting favorite mint-jelly-and-cheese cracker sandwiches.

Frank looked at the tray and probably noticed she'd only brought one drink. He said, "I'm good right now, Maxey. Why don't you see if your sister would like it?"

Maxey just kept shoving the glass up to him. "Oh, Effie doesn't like iced tea. *Children* like juice better."

"I love iced tea!" I said, sticking out a dirty hand.

She flashed me a look.

Frank took it from her and handed it to me.

I gulped some down. "Thanks, Maxey!"

"You're very welcome," she said, probably wishing she could smack me.

Frank turned to her. "Want to come help us?"

She looked down at her dress. "Oh! I wish I could, but I've got a ton of reading to do for school. I thought I'd come out here and do it, though. I love studying outdoors," she lied. "Under this beautiful sky God painted for us."

I whacked at a big bunch of crabgrass. I never thought there could be anything worse than having to live with Bosszilla.

But St. Maxey in Love was getting to be really, really hard to swallow.

Chapter 15

I fished for a big piece of ice from my Super Seismic Limeade and rubbed it over the super seismic blister on my hand.

Nit peered down at it. "Ef, you should have worn garden gloves."

"It's okay," I said. Nothing could ruin how happy I was to be sitting here with Nit and Aurora at Big Arlene's Ice Scream Shop. We'd all had burgers and fries, then pooled our money and shared the Triple Towers Monster Sundae. It's so good it makes your teeth ache.

I sank back against the green leather booth where we were having our Sunday reunion. Most parents didn't mind kids coming here without them because Big Arlene didn't tolerate any funny business. She was a plus-sized woman with no children of her own who used to be in the army, just like Principal Obermeyer. But they don't know each other because I checked.

"I feel like some zombie that's just been let out in the daylight," Aurora said. "My mom wouldn't even let me out of the house until today. She got so much work from Mr. Giles! I had to do all my regular schoolwork, then homework, plus tons of extra housework. Since my mom had to take the week off work, she decided we should do spring cleaning." She took a slurp of her drink and then slammed it down on the table. "This has been the crummiest week ever."

"Didn't you go over to Sam Houston's one night to watch the sixth graders play ball?" Nit asked. "I thought you said you did in your letter."

"Oh, yeah, that's right. My folks let me go because it was a school event. But I had to come right home afterward."

"I was going crazy not being able to talk to you guys!" I said, looking at them. "That was a very sneaky trick our mothers played. I couldn't believe they came up with that."

"Well," Nit said, dipping a giant steak-cut French fry into a pool of ketchup, "they had a little help."

"What do you mean?" I asked.

"Queen Maxine and Princess Tagalong!"

I sucked in my breath. "Them?"

"Who else?" she asked. "Once Maxey heard you got grounded from Aurora, but not from me, she raced to the phone and called Phil, who told my mom that I really should be grounded from you, since you were turning out to be a bad influence."

"I'm going to get her!"

Nit made wet little circles on the table with her finger. "What's happening with Chip?"

Aurora sighed. "Well, he had to go to juvenile court the other day, and since it's the first time for him, he'll probably just get put on probation. But the two older Turner kids are in *big* trouble because they've been arrested a few other times. They might get sent to one of those camps for really bad teenage boys. I think the youngest one will just get probation like Chip."

"Are your parents still thinking about sending him away to military school?"

She nodded.

The door to Big Arlene's swung open and some older girls came in. One of them dribbled a basketball all the way in.

"Park it!" Big Arlene barked at her.

"Yes, ma'am!" She saluted. She set it on the seat of the booth next to ours. "Triboni!" she said. "Keep an eye on my ball, will ya?"

"Sure," Aurora said.

The girl took a giant wad of pink gum out of her mouth and planted it on the tabletop with her thumb. "Watch my gum, too."

"Yeah, whatever," Aurora said.

She gave me and Nit a look. "Hope you girls remembered to say your prayers before you ate."

"Do you know her?" I whispered to Aurora.

"Yeah, sort of," Aurora said. "Her name is Fancy. She's a sixth grader over at Sam Houston's."

Nit did a double take. "Sixth grade? She looks like she's in high school!"

"I know!" Aurora said. "Big, huh? She's got a full rack already."

"A full rack of what?" I asked.

"Breasts," Nit explained.

"Oh." I blushed. Was I ever going to catch up on all the secret things that girls are supposed to know? I dug around in my drink with my straw.

"What's going to happen next, Aurora? Did you and your parents think it over? I mean, well, are you coming back to school tomorrow?"

The door flew open with a bang. Aurora's eyes narrowed and went tense.

"Hey, Marcus, check this *out*," a boy yelled.

Nit and I whipped around. A whole gang of boys from St. Dom's came pouring in the door. They took one look at Aurora and started in.

"Woof-woof! Arf-arf-arf!"

"Marcus, don't worry, man, we won't let the big bad fourth grader get you." That cracked them all up, and they crowded around him, laughing.

"Shut your piehole, you idiots." Booger Boy shoved them away. He looked over at us and gave us a wave. "Just ignore them. They're fools. We miss seeing you at school, Triboni. You coming back or what?"

Aurora leapt from the table, or tried to. Nit and I threw ourselves on top of her and hung on for dear life.

Chapter 16

"GIRL FIGHT!" someone screamed.

"We're not fighting!" Nit yelled.

Nit and I hung on to Aurora like a couple of bear cubs while she climbed out of the booth, trying to peel us off of her.

"Let GO!" she yelled.

"Whoa! Look out, Marcus!" one of the boys called. "She's coming after you!"

"Aurora! Stop!" I begged. "You're only going to make things worse!"

Fancy planted herself right in front of Aurora. "Knock it off, Triboni! There's no fighting in here. You're gonna make Big Arlene mad."

Aurora stopped struggling, but her face was still very red.

"What's the problem?" Fancy asked. "Those boys bugging you?" She turned to give them a Look.

Aurora set her mouth in a hard line. She was so mad she wouldn't talk.

Nit and I jumped in, trying to explain.

"The two of them got into a fight last week at school and then—" Nit started.

"He's been leaving love notes in her desk and then he sent her a singing valentine," I explained.

"Wait a minute!" Booger Boy said, coming up next to Fancy. "I don't know what your beef is, Triboni. I've never left any notes in your desk, and I'm *not* the one that sent that singing valentine."

"Shut up, Marcus." She lunged toward him.

"Take it easy, Triboni," Fancy said.

"Fine, believe what you want," he said. "But if you're ever interested in the truth, you might want to ask Kayla about who sent it. And about who wanted to know what kind of Valentine candy you like. That's what I get for trying to be a nice guy and getting some info for her. Never again," he said. "I'm out of here." The door slammed behind him.

Kayla! What did she have to do with this?

Fancy walked over to the boys with her basketball under one arm. Quick as a flash, she bounced the ball off the head of the kid who had been doing most of the barking. "Now get out of here and leave me and my girls alone."

Big Arlene came out of the kitchen then, wiping her red hands on a big dish towel.

"What's all the ruckus out here? Can't even hear myself think over you kids."

It got real quiet, and the boys all turned and slunk out. Not even a final *woof* from any of them.

"We're cool," Fancy said. "Sorry 'bout that, Big A."

Fancy came over and gave Aurora a poke in the chest. "Save it for the court. See you at practice tomorrow. Three o'clock sharp! Don't be late!"

Nit and I shot a horrified look at Aurora.

A terrible feeling of déjà-voodoo shot right through me. Like a couple of months ago when Aurora double-crossed me and joined Kayla's Discovery Project team!

Nit broke in, "Uh, we don't get out of class until three-thirty, Aurora, remember? How are you going to get to a basketball practice by three?"

Fancy twirled her ball on the tip of her finger, spinning it faster and faster. "Easy, she just walks out of her last class at Sam Houston's and heads for the gym."

Aurora kept her eyes on the ball. Like she'd been hypnotized. Didn't say a word.

Chapter 17

The three of us walked over to Nit's from Big Arlene's, but we weren't talking.

At least, not yet.

When we got to Nit's place, we filed into her bedroom. Me and Nit sat on the bed and stared at Aurora, who got very interested in Nit's bookcase.

Someone started banging on Nit's bedroom door, and she yelled, "What?"

Phil, aka Princess Tagalong, stuck her head inside. She eyeballed me. "Oh, good, you're here too. Can I come in?"

"What *for*?"

Wow, this was impressive. Even if I had my own room, Maxey would never let a door stop her.

"C'mon," Phil said. "I need to talk to Effie, please?"

"Make it quick," Nit said.

Phil walked to the center of the room and looked around with a shudder. She looked up at the bunches of garlic that Nit had hung from the ceiling. "Doesn't this room just creep you guys out?"

Unlike Aurora's room, which is all pink, and mine, which is all bunnies, Nit's room is sort of, well, black. She has a giant cardboard stand-up of a pretty scary-looking vampire in the corner. But he's wearing Nit's Angel Scout beanie, so it's hard to get too worked up.

"No!" we said in unison.

"Whatever!" Phil said. "Effie, what is *up* with your sister?"

"How should I know? She's *your* best friend."

"Well, I thought so too, but . . ." She paused to inspect herself in the mirror on Nit's closet door.

"Is there a point to this?" Nit asked. "We're kind of busy."

"Well, I just called Maxey, and this is the third time this week she said she is too busy studying religion to talk, and just now, when I said good-bye, she said, 'God bless you.' "

Maxey was sailing right off the edge of the world.

"Maybe she has a brain tumor," Nit volunteered. "I read once that if you have a tumor in a certain place, it turns you kind of religious."

"Oh, good! I hope that's it. I'd hate to think she was really turning all freakish on me."

"It's just Frank," I said. "It'll wear off."

"Who's Frank?" Nit asked.

"Frank is their new man roommate," Phil crooned, giving me a secret look. Aurora turned to me, talking all of a sudden. "You have some guy living at your house now?"

"Yeah, I just didn't get a chance to tell you yet. I wasn't

keeping it a *secret* or anything. I don't keep *secrets* from my best friends." I gave her a pointed look. "But with all of us being grounded, I haven't even had a chance to tell you. My mom's old friend from college has moved in with us for a while. Just so he can do some yard work and fix a few things around the house."

Nit gave me a squint-eyed look, and I could tell she was putting some feelers out on this one. "Why would this guy make Maxey want to study religion and bless people?"

"Well, he's not much of a churchgoer, but he's still kind of holy—he's probably just rubbing off on her."

Phil purred, still in front of the mirror. "I wish he'd rub on me a little. He is capital *H* hot!"

Nit grabbed her big vampire book from the floor, and Phil jumped back a foot. "I'm leaving already! Don't hex me, you creepy little vampire witch!" The door slammed behind her.

"She is so ignorant," Nit said after she left. "You can't be a vampire and a witch at the same time."

"Doesn't matter," I said. "She's really scared of you! That is so cool."

"Do you like this guy, Frank?" Nit asked me, her antennae still out.

"No!" I said. "I wish he'd hurry up and leave."

"How come?" Aurora asked. "Is he mean to you or something?"

"No, not mean."

"Does he eat chips all over the couch and fart during football games? Man, I hate that," Aurora said.

"No, he's pretty quiet. But there's something funny about him."

Nit leaned in. "Like what?"

I shrugged. I didn't want Nit to start reading my mind like she does sometimes. Mom would be mad at me if anyone knew. "I don't know. Just funny."

Nit kept staring at me as if she knew I was holding back. I tried to fill my mind with something else.

"Look!" I said. "Can we get off Frank? I think we have something slightly more important to talk about." I crossed my arms and turned toward Aurora. "Like how you've decided to go to Sam Houston's without even telling us! How could you do that?"

"I'm sorry!" she said. "But I haven't been able to talk to you guys this week, and I couldn't stay home forever. Mom had to go back to work, and I just don't want to go back to St. Dominic's. I'm sick of kids staring at me, talking about me, barking at me. And I want to play ball! I love basketball. When I went to that game the other night and watched Fancy's team play, I knew I had to play with them. It's all I can think about and dream about. And most all the girls on the team look like me. They got big feet, big hands, big everything. I just blend right in. That's all I want. To *blend* in. What's wrong with that?" Aurora's teeth pinned her bottom lip to keep it from trembling. "We'll still be friends."

I really, truly wanted to be mad at her. But I could feel myself going soft. I was starting to understand that going through puberty in fourth grade was probably as hard for Aurora as having a crook for a dad was for me. And maybe as hard as it had been for Nit when everyone used to ignore her or make fun of her.

All of a sudden I could see that the three of us were different in ways that you really didn't want to be. Since we'd become best friends, though, a lot of things had gotten easier. But right now, things were very hard for Aurora.

Being a good friend meant we had to look out for each other when things got hard. Even if we didn't like it one bit.

"Just think," I said. "You don't have to wear those itchy old uniforms anymore!"

Nit smiled at me with her eyes. "Right! And you don't have to pack a smelly old sandwich to take every day. Sam Houston's probably has a cafeteria—I think all the public schools do. They might even have a soda machine!"

Aurora unpinned her lip and swiped at her nose.

"No more religion homework!" I cheered.

"No more chocolate to sell!" Nit jumped in.

Aurora laughed at that. "I do like the chocolate."

"Good thing you have two best friends in Catholic school that will keep you supplied," I said.

She grinned. "It sure is!"

Chapter 18

There are worse things than living with the bossiest girl in town.

One, for example, is having a runaway priest camping out in your mother's office and leaving man hair in the downstairs shower drain.

I know that thinking a priest is a big creep is probably a *very bad* sin, but I can't help it. It's not the priest part about Frank I don't like—I wouldn't like him if he was a fireman, a rock star, or the guy with the muscles that scoops the ice cream at Big Arlene's.

Mom is always telling us how important good communication is, so I was making her a list of all the things I can't stand about Frank. I wanted to have it ready before the Team Meeting. Maybe she would ask him to move out afterward, and we could go back to our regular lives starting Monday. That would be awesome.

10 EXCELLENT REASONS WHY FRANK SHOULD LEAVE

1. He's made a terrible mess in the backyard.
2. He drinks a LOT of grapefruit juice.
3. Neighbors might think he and Mom are up to monkey business and they're not married.
4. He is making Maxey act like a freak.
5. He doesn't go to Mass and is setting a terrible example for us.
6. He is taking up a parking space on our street. What if an ambulance or fire truck needed that space?
7. He doesn't like regular French toast. That's our Family Tradition.
8. Once I had to go to the bathroom downstairs, and he was already in there, and I heard if you hold it too long, you could get a hernia.
9. He is not kind to gophers.
10. ~~He is making Mom act kinda weird.~~

I figured I better scratch the last one. Mom might not like that. But it was true. She wasn't acting all religious, but she was always cutting up around him. The two of them spent a lot of time laughing. And I noticed she wasn't wearing her mother ponytail like she usually did. Instead, she wore her hair down, and I caught her putting on lip gloss after dinner one night.

Frank had no right to come into our house and hog all her attention. Just because we had a man vacancy in our house didn't mean he could just park himself right in the middle of it. I liked it empty. Well, maybe I didn't like it, but I was trying to get used to it. I still missed my grandpa so much! But having Frank around was making me remember things about my dad. Like how he'd look in the morning before he shaved and the sound of his stubble when he'd rub it. Frank's big shiny man shoes smelled just like my dad's. And Frank was always whistling around the house and out back like Dad did, which I'd forgotten all about. It made me want to throw something at him when I heard it, so he'd stop.

Worst of all, Mom was falling for Frank, and God would not like that.

I folded my list quick when I heard Maxey come up the stairs and stuck it under my leg. At least, I thought it was Maxey. She didn't clomp up the stairs as often anymore. Sometimes she walked like an altar girl—all serious and devoted-looking.

"Mom says twenty minutes until dinner." She paused at my bed.

I waited for her to finish her sentence like she usually did, with something like "So go wash your filthy paws" or "Do you *ever* brush your teeth?"

Instead, she just laid her hand on top of my head. I ducked, swatting it away. "Cut it out."

"I was blessing you! Frank blessed me earlier and told me to pass it on. He said you don't have to be a priest to give a blessing. So I blessed Mom and Pretty Girl, and sent one to Dad and Grandpa, too."

"It's not like Frank is going to start dating you, you know, if you act all holy," I said.

Maxey smiled at me like I was a cute chipmunk. "Of course not. Priests don't date."

"Don't be so sure he's even a priest," I told her. "If he is, he is the worst one ever. Instead of helping the poor and saying Mass, he's hiding out here making you act like a wacko and flirting with our mother!"

"He isn't flirting with Mom. He told me all about his vow of chastity. He's married to God, you know. That's what that ring on his finger is from. An ordination is like a wedding."

"Then why is Mom acting so funny and girly?"

"She's very happy to have a man in the house—and I am too. You might show a little more gratitude."

"I'll show you some gratitude when he goes back to where he came from."

Maxey dropped down on the bed next to me. She lowered her voice. "I heard him on the phone with his monsignor the other day."

"Really? What did he say?"

"He was telling him he needed some more time. He kept saying that over and over."

"Then what?"

"Then Mom snuck up on me and gave me the business about eavesdropping." She picked at the polish on her nails. "I want you to be nicer to him. I don't want him leaving here to go stay somewhere else. Do you want me to help you say some special prayers so that you're not so nasty?"

"You're freaking Phil out, you know."

"That's her problem," she said. "Hey, Ef, look at that!" she said, pointing out our window.

I turned and Maxey snatched my list from under my leg. She jumped off the bed and opened it.

"Give that to me!" I yelled. "It's personal!"

Her face grew dark as she read it. "You are so ungrateful! I can't believe you. What were you planning to do with this?" She held it high over her head so I couldn't get it back.

"It's mine!"

"You writing this for Mom?" she asked, waving it over our heads. "Do you know how bad it will make her feel that you don't like the best friend she's got? What if she made you a list of the reasons she couldn't stand your creepy little friends? How would you like that?"

I leapt onto the bed, then dove over her and grabbed it out of her hand as we tumbled to the floor together.

"Dinner, girls!" Mom called up the stairs.

Maxey glared at me as she picked herself up. "This is not over!"

Chapter 19

Frank was still there for breakfast on Monday, sucking down our grapefruit juice and jumping around getting Mom coffee. And getting in my way while I tried to pack my lunch. Hopefully, this was his last meal. I'd put my "9 Excellent Reasons Why Frank Should Leave" list in an envelope and stuck it in the special book Mom reads at night before she goes to sleep. I did feel kind of bad about giving it to her, but it was the right thing to do. She just couldn't see what a bad influence he was.

The Team Meeting had been a bust and so boring it nearly put me into a coma. Maxey hung on Frank's every word. He was going on and on about the immigrants and how most Americans didn't appreciate how good we had it. And how charity wasn't enough, and we all needed to work for social justice.

Mom tried to draw me into the conversation and asked me if I knew the difference between pity and compassion.

Maxey waved her arm like she was in class, but Mom wanted to know what I thought. I wanted to tell her that I thought the Team Meeting was much better BF (Before Frank), when it was for complaining about your sister, and maybe making brownies afterward. But I just sighed and said that if you have compassion for someone, you would walk a mile in their shoes. If you pity them, you wouldn't put on their shoes for anything.

Mom and Frank had both smiled, even though I didn't mean to be funny. Frank patted my arm and said, "I like that. I'll have to remember it."

Just then Pretty Girl came hurrying into the kitchen where we were having breakfast like she was late for an appointment. She vaulted into Frank's lap. We were all shocked, except for Frank. He patted her and didn't get his eyes scratched out or anything! He even leaned over and kissed her on her head. Unbelievable!

For one thing, nineteen-year-old cats are too old to be hurrying and jumping anywhere. And since Grandpa died, Pretty Girl hasn't let anyone hold her. Frank was petting her like it was a regular thing. He told us that she had been coming in and sleeping on the pull-out couch with him at night.

I glared at her.

Frank poured his second glass of juice, and I politely cleared my throat and looked at Mom. She stepped on my foot under the table.

"Effie, how about I give you a ride to school today?" Mom asked. "I'd like to talk to you about something."

I shot a look at Maxey. She sucked in her breath like she was ready to pitch a fit. Instead, she gave us all a polite smile and got back to eating.

"Sure!" I darted another look at Maxey. "Can we stop at Eller's and buy a doughnut for my snack? I have money left from my allowance."

Maxey picked up the box of Organic Wheat-Os and started reading the back of it. She loved Eller's doughnuts. This was bound to make her crack.

I waited. Nothing. Oh, man, she was a brick.

"Hey, Max, how about I give you a lift to school this morning?" Frank asked. "I need to go to the library, and you can show me where it is before I drop you off."

Maxey popped out from behind the cereal box. "Sure!" She grinned. She made a quick cross over her bowl and ran upstairs to get her stuff for school.

"Did she just bless her cereal bowl?" Mom asked.

"Mmm-hmm," he mumbled, his mouth full.

• • •

"He's having the worst influence on her," I told Mom as she ground the stick thing on our VW into reverse. "She's acting all holy, but it's the bad kind. It's mean holy, where you just want everyone to do what you say. I wouldn't mind so much if it was making her act nice."

"Ef, be patient with her. She doesn't know how to act around a man. She's trying very hard to please him. Can you understand that?"

"Why can't she just be a normal kid?"

"Maybe she thinks normal isn't good enough. Look, cupcake, she's doing the best she can. Try to look at things a little bit deeper, will you?"

"This could ruin her popularity if she starts acting all St. Maxey at school."

"That is not at the top of my list of worries for her."

"Well, I'm just giving you a friendly warning."

"You seem to be full of 'friendly' warnings these days. I got your list of reasons you think Frank should move out."

"Good! When are you going to talk to him?"

"Effie, I think you may be overreacting a little. I know having a man in the house after all these years is a bit strange. It's strange for me, too. But I feel it's the right thing to do. Do you think you could find some room in your heart for him too?"

"I can find some room in my heart, I just don't know why I have to find room in my house! It's not working out."

"Well, I went through your list very carefully last night, and I think we can solve your concerns. I really don't think parking is a problem, and I'll buy extra juice if you're truly worried. I'm confident Frank will finish the yard—"

"Are you in *love* with him, Mom?" I blurted.

"Is that what you're worried about?" She turned to look at me.

"Well, are you? You act like you might be."

She didn't say anything for a minute as she cranked the steering wheel to get us out of the driveway. "I loved Frank in that way once, but it was a very long time ago. And God was always the love of his life."

"Well, I don't know if you've noticed, but I think he and

God are having . . . marriage problems. What if he wants to stop being a priest and be your husband?"

"That's never going to happen, Ef."

"I don't know how you can say that," I said. "I bet you never thought Dad was going to go to the slammer. You don't know *everything*."

"I know that I would never try to steal someone from the church," she said. "Besides, I'm too busy for a husband. They're a lot of work. I'd rather have a wife."

"*Mom!*" I said. "You're not allowed! Sister Emmanuel told us in class that a man has to marry a woman and vice versa."

"Effie, you have my permission to ignore whatever Sister Emmanuel tells you about marriage, and dating . . . and, well, pretty much anything else she says about men and women. God made all kinds of people, and it isn't our place to judge anyone."

"Mom, is the reason you don't want to marry Frank because you're a *lesbian*? Maxey told me a lot of lady coaches are."

I didn't tell her what some neighbor boys told Maxey— that the reason Dad went nuts and started stealing was because Mom was dating one of the nuns at her high school!

"No, I don't think so," she said, turning into the driveway of Eller's Doughnuts. "But some days it seems like a very good idea."

I sighed and dug for my Hello Kitty change purse in my backpack. "It isn't easy being a kid in this family, you know."

She patted my knee. "I know, Ef. Buy me a doughnut?"

Chapter 20

I hated looking at Aurora's old desk where she used to sit. Missed seeing the basketball that was always tucked under her seat. Missed the smell of her even—sort of sporty and sweaty and sugary. It made me feel like bawling. She'd been gone a whole week. Nit and I tried to be very positive when we talked to her on the phone, or sent her an e-mail, but we weren't happy. It felt like somebody had died. Aurora, on the other hand, sounded very happy. She got to wear pants and sometimes even shorts to school. And nobody had barked at her at Sam Houston's.

I tried to concentrate on what Mr. Giles was saying about the Continental Divide, but I couldn't keep my mind on it. A tightly packed tiny paper square came sailing my way and bopped me on the forehead. I swept it off my desk, dropped it into my hand, and held it tight. These days, I was super-careful. I still was trying to get back on Mr. Giles's good side.

When Mr. Giles went to the door to talk to the attendance monitor, I opened it. It was from Nit, of course. But she'd written it in text message, so it took me a while to decode it. She was learning text so she could read Phil's private messages. *Donal sed Booger boi wntz 2 MEt us Bhind d Dumpstr @ lch.* I folded her note back up and stuck it inside my shoe. Didn't want to take any chances. If I made Mr. Giles mad, I might end up in Sister Emmanuel's office again. Not to mention big trouble with Mom. She'd sentence me to more yard work with Frank. I blew out a fake sneeze to get Nit's attention and she turned around. I gave her a thumbs-up.

• • •

Donal was waiting by the classroom door as we filed out. "Whatcha think the Boger Boy wants from you?"

I shrugged. "What's it to you?"

"Right, I'll come along, then," he said, falling in behind us. "He might be up to no good. Be wide with that one!"

"What is he saying?" I asked Nit.

"He said we need to be careful."

I turned to Donal. "I'm not afraid of that maggot. Anyway," I said, "this is sort of private. But thanks for giving us the message and all."

"He's a blackguard, that one," he said, trailing in our wake.

"That means he's up to no good," Nit translated.

"Oh," I said. "Well, Donal's got his number, all right." But Donal couldn't take a hint if you put it on a flashing billboard. Ever since Aurora left, he'd been dogging me and Nit. Couldn't tell you why.

Booger Boy was leaned up against the stinky Dumpster, eating a tuna sandwich. A bunch of the younger kids were standing around, all jacked up about something. He was taking quarters from them and shoving them into his pocket.

"Hold on, girls, I'll be right with you. Anyone else?" he asked. "Simon! Scram! You didn't pay. You don't get to watch. Okay, everyone ready?"

The boys shouted, "Yes!"

He looked over at the two of us. "Well, you two didn't pay, but that's okay. And for you, too, Lucky Charm," he said to Donal. "Thanks for bringing the wee fine lasses with ya!" He did a bad Irish jig and then laughed.

Donal's ears turned pink.

"Okay, it's showtime!" Marcus handed his sandwich over to Donal. "Hold that a sec." He reached into his coat pocket and pulled out a small can.

Cat food? I looked at Nit and shrugged.

"Okay, get closer, so you can see," he said.

The kids scrunched in around him.

"This one here happens to be my favorite flavor—Chicken Hearts and Liver Feast in Gravy. Yum!"

"Ewww, that's so sick!" one of the boys cried.

Booger Boy grinned and popped the top off. He pulled a plastic spoon out of his back pocket and shoved it into the can. He smacked his lips.

"Anyone want a taste?"

"NO!" the boys yelled.

"You're *not* going to eat that!" Nit yelped.

He didn't answer, just opened wide and spooned it in. "Mmmmm," he moaned through closed lips.

"All of it!" his audience screamed.

He kept on going until he'd eaten the very last bit. Then he ran his finger around the inside to get the last morsels and licked it with a smack.

"You are SICK!" I yelled. "And a terrible example to these kids!"

He let out a big burp.

The kids screamed and started dancing around and punching each other.

"Now, who wants to smell my breath—it's on the house!"

"That is manky!" Donal said, shuddering.

Marcus licked his fingers and smacked his lips. "We need to talk. Scram, fellas." He gestured to his audience. He grabbed his sandwich back from Donal and took a big bite.

While the kids ran off, Donal cozied right up.

"Donal?" I asked. "Do you mind?"

"Not at all. Go on with you."

Nit nudged me. "It's all right."

She turned to Marcus. "What did you want to see us about?"

I broke in. "Maybe you'd like to run a few more kids out of school, huh?" Even if Aurora did want to go to Sam Houston's to save her parents money, I still thought it was mostly his fault!

"Just wondered if you'd talked to Kayla yet," he said. "I'm pretty tired of carrying her rap."

"I asked her and she just laughed at me. Said she had plenty of more important things to spend her money on than a singing valentine for her '*ex*-best friend.' " She'd nearly spit on me.

Booger Boy pulled out a piece of paper. "Well, you might want to take a look at this."

Nit and Donal crowded around. It was the words to the

singing valentine written in big block letters. "This doesn't prove anything. You could have written it. Kayla's handwriting is fancier than this," I said.

"What else do you notice about it?" he said.

Nit looked up at him. "Purple ink, one of those sparkly pens."

"That's a pen for the lasses," Donal said. "No boy would carry that."

Marcus reached into his back pocket and pulled out a pen. "Like this one?"

I grabbed it. My heart started banging. It had a label that read "Property of Kayla Quintana." Kayla labeled everything on her desk and in her desk.

Donal shook his head. "The bowsie. She framed ya!"

Chapter 21

Frank was the only one home when I got there. He was in the kitchen drinking a lot of our special bottled water when I went in. He was wearing a Notre Dame T-shirt that was very dirty and had giant sweat spots on the front and back. Ick. Like he'd sprung a leak.

"Hi, Ef!" he said, wiping his mouth.

"H'lo." I set down my backpack. I took a banana from the fruit bowl and started to leave.

"How was school today?"

That was my mother's question to ask, not his. I stopped and turned around, though.

"Terrible!" That would put him off.

He took the banana from my hand and started to peel it. Now he was taking the very food right out of my mouth!

"Here you go, Ef." He handed it back. "A girl needs to eat. Now, tell me what was so terrible about your day." He pulled out a chair from the kitchen table.

I plopped down and took a big bite. I chewed for a minute and took a sniff of him while I was at it. For all the yard work he did, he never got stinky. It was a mystery.

I wondered if it was a priest thing. Maybe since you couldn't get married and all that, God decided he owed you a favor and took away stuff like body odor, maybe bad breath, too. I'd check with Nit. She knew all kinds of stuff.

While I was chewing, Frank got up and poured me a glass of milk. Then he reached into the high cupboard above the fridge, where Mom hid the chocolate chips from me. He dropped a few into my milk, then plopped it down in front of me. I stopped chewing. How the heck did he know I did that when I thought no one was looking?

"My mom used to hide the chocolate chips from me, too," he said.

I took a drink of chocolate-chip milk and didn't say anything. This wasn't confession, after all.

"What happened at school today?"

"Well, for one, Aurora Triboni is still not there, and nothing is the same without her. I hate it. And there was a rumor going around after lunch today that Maxey was actually *praying* during grace before lunch!"

"Not good, right?" he asked.

"You're about to ruin her for good," I said. "Not that I care what happens to her, really, but it's hard enough living in this family as it is." I drained my milk, whacking the chocolate chips from the bottom.

"It is hard on you, isn't it, Ef?" His voice was soft. Like the way Principal Obermeyer talked to me—her questions were like invitations.

"It's very hard! And completely unfair. Me and Mom and Maxey don't deserve any of it. A lot of people in this town would be pretty happy if we all fell right off the face of the earth. Like what Dad did is our fault. I wish we didn't have to be so poor. Did you know that Mom and Grandpa gave up just about every extra cent they had in the world to try to pay some of the families back? No one ever mentions that. So we'll never be able to get a new car or have anything nice or sort of fancy because of him."

I stopped to catch my breath and waited for him to say something like "But you have each other" or "Blessed are the poor."

"I'm so sorry, Effie."

Pretty Girl came hurrying in and leapt into Frank's lap. He rubbed her ears, and she had that look on her face that she did when Grandpa used to hold her. Like she'd just had an entire bath in cream.

"I miss Grandpa!"

"He was such a great guy."

I squinted at him. "You knew him?"

"Sure I did. Your mom used to take me to your grandma and grandpa's house for some of the holidays and school breaks. I loved going there. They always made me feel at home, and fed me until I nearly popped."

"I never met my grandma."

"You got your gorgeous red hair from her."

I nodded and fiddled with the buttons on my sweater.

"You can't take his place," I said. "I won't let you."

"Your dad's?" he asked. He moved his hand toward mine, and I pulled it off the table quick.

I stood up from the table, held myself tall. "You can try all you like, but you can't win my mom back!"

"Effie, I promise you, I won't even try."

I moved away from the table. "Just because Maxey fell for you, don't think I'm going to. I would never, ever want you for my father."

"I'm not trying to be," he said. "I'd like to be your friend."

I slammed my glass on the counter. I was so done with this conversation.

"Why would I believe you?" I shot out of the room.

• • •

It was dust that called me into Frank's room—really. Mom might have forgotten to clean up in there. And he was too busy with the labyrinth to take care of it. I waited until everyone was away from the house. Some people are very sensitive to dust particles, and you shouldn't stir them up when they are around.

I hadn't really been in Mom's office since it was turned into Frank's bedroom when he moved in two years ago. Well, it wasn't two years ago, not even a month, but it felt longer—way longer.

It was tidier than when Mom had the run of it. He was sleeping on her pull-out couch, but he made it back to the couch during the day. The blankets and sheets were folded up on one end. I picked up the pillow and smelled it. I admit it. I'm very curious about the way men smell. Frank's rosary was underneath where the pillow had been. It was a big brown one, plain. Not with glittery beads on it like the ones Maxey and I had. I smelled that, too. I don't know why. I'm just a sniffer, I guess.

I tucked it back under his pillow and went over to the desk to dust and snoop. Mom had cleared all her stuff off of it so he could put his things out. I ran the rag over it, but it was really clean already.

He had all his special things lined up very neat. There was a small statue of the Blessed Mother, his car keys, a very fancy pen, sunglasses, and his shaving kit. And a leather book with some zippered compartments that looked sort of interesting. It was like a man diary with a calendar in it, and some letters, his cell phone bill, and some pictures. I shut it and put it down. That would be really bad of me to go through it, and I had to think that God was watching.

I opened it again anyway. Shut it fast.

Effie! This is bad.

I opened it one last time. Looked under *M* in the address book. There we were—the Maloneys—all listed under Mom's name, and our birthdays, too. Dad's name was there, but he'd crossed him out. I bet that made Frank pretty happy to do that.

I ran my finger over Dad's name, as if I could magically unerase him and he might show up. Not that I really wanted him to. Well, maybe sometimes I did. I missed having his big shoes that I could clomp around in. I liked him tickling me. He knew all the best spots to get me going. And I liked when he'd fix my hair because he didn't brush as hard as Mom did.

I'm not sure what else dads are supposed to do. Mow the lawn, make money, and barbecue, I think. Mom pretty much knows how to do all that. We're kind of set.

I decided I'd rather have Grandpa back if I could make somebody magically reappear. I would have gotten him to throw Frank out right away. I could just tell he was out to break my mother's heart. Even though she said she wasn't in love with him, I wasn't sure I believed her.

There was a funny little bulge in one of the side pockets of the book, and I dug my finger into it. I pulled out a small gold key. But it was nothing like I'd ever seen. It had these swirly engravings on it, and a big red ruby right smack in the middle.

It sure as heck wasn't the spare key to his car, or even his house key. It looked like the key to some millionaire's house or a very fancy box.

This did not make sense. Or maybe it made perfect sense.

Mom had done it again. She'd let another fox into the henhouse. Frank had to be a crook. Priests take a vow of poverty. Frank was holding out on the church. He was holding the key to some serious dough.

But this time I wasn't going to let us get duped. I studied the key, both sides, looking for clues. I shut his book and put it right where I found it. Made sure nothing looked out of order. I made a quick apology to the statue of the Blessed Mother that was staring at me and dropped the key deep into the pocket of my shorts.

Every now and then the thief gene I had inherited came in handy, I supposed. But it gave me the wicked willies. I did not want to be the apple that fell from Dad's tree.

I hoped I could control it. If not, maybe I had some Robin Hood in me.

I could steal for the poor, instead of from them.

They might have nicer prisons for people who did that. I could hope.

Chapter 22

"What do you mean you don't *want* to have a slumber party?" Mom asked Maxey. "You've been asking for one for nearly—ever!"

We were in the kitchen cleaning up after dinner. Except for Frank, who was baking cookies and making more messy dishes for us. He looked quite thrilled with himself too.

"I just changed my mind, that's all," Maxey said, drying a plate and looking all innocent.

I narrowed my eyes at her. Fishy.

"Did you and Phil have a fight?" Mom asked.

She shrugged. "No, it's just . . . the girls in my class are all so shallow." She darted a look at Frank, who was checking the oven.

"Okay, if that's how you feel about it," Mom said. "I'm just surprised. You've worked so hard on pulling up your religion grade. When I talked to Sister today, she couldn't stop praising your work."

"Maybe Effie would like to have a slumber party," Maxey suggested.

Mom and I nearly had to sit down at that. I was ready to call 911 and have the crime lab take DNA from her. This could not be my sister.

"I want one!" I yelled.

"See, Mom?" Maxey said. "Let Effie have it. It would be nice for her and her little friends."

"Little?" I huffed.

"I just meant 'younger.' "

"Please, please, please, Mom?" I begged. "I really need to have a slumber party right now. All the girls at school miss Aurora. And we don't want her to forget about us!"

"Let her have one, Mom," Maxey said. "I'll help. And Frank will too, I know," she said, her eyes getting shiny.

"Well, all right, I suppose," Mom said.

"Yeess!" I screamed.

"Maxey, why don't you invite Phil to sleep over that night, though?" Mom said. "She can help out, and it will be more fun for you to have someone your own age here."

"I suppose," she said. "But could I have something else for bringing up my grade?"

"Aha!" Mom said, snapping a dish towel at her. "I knew there had to be a 'something else.' "

Frank came over with a plate of steaming peanut butter cookies and offered it to me. "No thanks," I said.

Mom took two.

I was dying to hear what Maxey wanted. "Well, what is it?"

Maxey leaned over and whispered something in Mom's ear. Mom rolled her eyes, then laughed. "Really? *That's* what you want?"

Maxey grinned and nodded.

"I don't know, Max."

"C'mon, please, Mom?"

"You promise me you'll read the instructions very carefully?"

"Yes! Yes!" Maxey started twirling around the kitchen.

"You're killing us!" Frank said. "Tell."

"It's a secret," Maxey said. "For now."

"What about my slumber party, Mom?" I butted in. "Is this a for-sure-yes or a maybe-yes?"

She threw up her hands. "Well, I suppose it's a yes-yes!"

I hugged her around the neck. "Thanks, Mom! I can't believe it! Wait until I tell Nit and Aurora! How many can I invite? Can we have those little pizzas for snacks and rent as many videos as we want? I'm going to wear my new slippers from Christmas, and I'll share my nail polish and maybe we can make those funny ice cubes with the fake spiders in them!"

I ran right over to the refrigerator and added it to my list of lucky things:

8. I get to have my first slumber party!!

"I think we should ask each of the girls to bring some canned food for the homeless," Maxey said. "You know, instead of presents. It's not like it's Effie's birthday or anything."

"NO!" I shouted.

"Well, fine," she said, tossing her hair over her shoulder in her usual snotty way.

I should have known this wasn't going to be the kind of slumber party you read about in *American Girl* magazine. Not when you're harboring a runaway priest, have a religious freak for a sister, and a prayer park is being built in your backyard.

I really, really should have given up the plan right then.

But I'm a sucker for a party.

• • •

Since it wasn't my birthday, we decided to have a St. Patrick's Day slumber party. It was my great idea to have it the Friday after St. Patrick's Day because then all the decorations would be marked down 75 percent. Mom said we could serve all green food, and I said that was okay as long as it wasn't vegetables. The kids would never forgive me if we served broccoli, asparagus, and peas. Frank said he was going to dye some tortillas green. I gave Mom a secret look like I might be choking, and she said we could worry about the menu later.

Nit and I made green and white polka-dot invitations with pink real-ribbon bows on the top. Nit wanted to put big, creepy snakes on them, like the kind St. Patrick drove out of Ireland, but I talked her out of it. Nit was the best, but she still had a freak streak.

I wanted everything to be perfect, totally normal.

Miss Effeline Maloney hereby invites you to
a Special St. Patrick's Day Slumber Party

DATE: Friday, March 21
TIME: 7:00 p.m. for Irish pizza and shamrock cake
ENDS: After breakfast the next day!
DON'T FORGET: Pajamas, pillow, sleeping bag
or just a blanket is fine
DO NOT BRING: A boy, a present, any pets,
or a cell phone that plays the kind of loud music
that drives my mother nuts.
Special Guest: Aurora Triboni
(Two adults in charge; one is just my mom's friend,
not her boyfriend.)

RSVP to Effie at 555-2356

Chapter 23

I was inviting every girl in my class, not like some of the kids, who had parties and invited only the people they liked. I'd never been invited to any of those, but you always heard about them. The kids would talk about them in big loud whispers that you couldn't miss hearing. For days before the party, even after I knew the invitations had gone out, I'd try being supernice to the girl who was having the party, in case she might change her mind at the very last minute. Then when I didn't get invited, I'd go around checking my breath all week, even though I knew deep down that the only thing wrong with me was my father the crook.

I wasn't inviting any boys. Not even Becca's twin brother, Bryce. The two of them hardly took a breath without each other, but who wanted a bunch of farty boys running around in their pajamas? They'd throw chips and see who could burp out their name the best.

It really chapped my hide to invite Kayla, who was such a double- and triple-crosser, but we were working on a plan to get her back for how she tried to embarrass Aurora with the singing valentine. Nit thought we should wait until Angel Scout Camp, when we'd have a whole week to lay a big trap for her. Nit said, too, that people reap what they sow, which means if you drop some stinkplant seeds around, you get a whole crop of it. She said it wouldn't surprise her if something bad happened to Kayla before we even got to her!

We were still trying to decide what activities we were going to have at the party. I knew from reading magazines that the activities were Very Important. I wanted to decorate T-shirts with glitter and fake jewels; Nit wanted to try to contact Marie Antoinette with a Ouija board; and when I asked Aurora, she said we could all play basketball. The only person who didn't have an opinion was Maxey, but she was probably hoping we could rebaptize a few kids.

Frank decided he needed to get the labyrinth done by the party, and so he was outside from the crack of dawn until late at night, putting all the stones and steps in place.

I made Mom promise me that Frank would not make the girls at my party walk the labyrinth. I'd never, ever live that down. She assured me he wouldn't. She said he just wanted the yard to look nice.

Mom bought Maxey and me brand-new pajamas. I got green and white polka dots, and Maxey got white, probably because she thought it would make her look more like an angel.

Brother.

I hinted around to Mom that maybe she could get one of those fancy mother nightgowns with the skinny straps, but she said she'd freeze to death. Or she might slide right off the bed. She slept in a big basketball jersey with cutoff sweatpants for her bottoms. Which was usually fine with me since I didn't want Frank thinking impure thoughts about her.

She said that lots of mothers didn't sleep in fancy night-gowns and that I shouldn't worry so much about what other people thought.

I didn't mind so much about what people thought, it was what they would say. I wanted the girls in my class to come over and see how nice and regular we were.

Well, nice, at least.

• • •

When I got home from school, Frank was out running, so I went to the backyard to check on how things were going. It didn't even look like our yard anymore. All the weeds were gone, and he'd trimmed the bushes and trees so it was a lot sunnier. Mom said he'd even fixed the old broken sprinklers that Dad had put in, so we could water again. I wondered if this was how the yard used to look before Dad left. But some things were just a big blank in my mind.

There were still a lot of holes that Frank was working on where he'd taken out some dead bushes. I stared down into them. They were really deep. Frank sure had been working hard. And it wasn't like Mom had begged him to do it. He just started digging away. He'd had to wipe out all the gopher tunnels too.

Dig, dig, dig. Day after day. Maybe he should give up being a priest and become a professional digger. Or a pirate.

A big jolt went right through me and almost tumped me over. How could I have been so stupid? He'd been out there digging for weeks. It wasn't about the labyrinth! That was his cover. Frank was either looking for something or burying something. And if he was looking for something in our backyard, it must be something he thought Dad had buried! Maybe some of the money Dad had embezzled. What if Dad and his partner didn't really lose it all in the stock market? Maybe my dad hid some!

My mind raced at light speed. What if Frank had gone to visit my dad in prison, and Dad had told him about the money? But why would Dad tell him? That didn't make sense.

I drew in my breath. Frank might have talked Dad into letting Frank hear his confession! That would be so wicked.

I made a meal of my lower lip. At times like this, I wished I could figure out things like Nit does. She always says anyone can do what she does if they just let their mind look at things from a lot of different angles. Think, Effie. What were the other possibilities? If he wasn't looking for something, maybe he was getting ready to bury something out here. Maybe he already had.

The gold key! It could be a key to a treasure box that he buried or was going to bury out here soon. I wondered what the treasure was. His inheritance money from his uncle Ruben?

Maybe it was money from the immigrants! I heard they

had to pay a lot of money to get people to bring them over the border. He could be bringing them over in his fancy car. No one would suspect a priest!

And now he was using our house as his cover. Frank probably figured that since we'd been so easily fooled by Dad, we were easy pickings.

He'd been working so hard—I bet he was getting ready to fly the coop.

You'd think this would be good news to me. But if Frank took off in the night, he was going to bust a couple of hearts. Maxey would get over it, but I don't know if Mom could survive another crook.

I had to do something! Fast.

• • •

Most girls would have run right into the house to tell their mother what they'd discovered. But not me. For one, Mom would never have believed it. She might even have gotten mad at me and canceled my slumber party. No way she would have wanted to hear that she'd ended up with another crook. I needed some hard evidence first. There was always the weensiest possibility that I was wrong.

Nah.

Back when Aurora still went to my school, I went to her house one afternoon to study. Aurora got bored with English and turned on the television in her room. She started watching one of those talk shows, the racy kind that Mom won't ever put on. There was this woman on the show who kept falling in love with convicts in prison. She'd date them while they were still locked up, and she even got married to three of them. Her sister and some of her friends wanted her to start dating and marrying regular guys. But the lady just kept shaking her head and saying that it was no use, because even if she quit them, they'd come find her. She said she was a "crook magnet."

What if Mom was one too? And what if it ran in the family, and me and Maxey ended up with criminals? I did not want to go to my first prom at Sing-Sing!

I needed to get some help, but not from Mom. I was so lucky to have two best friends to talk to. I'd have to be careful, though, that I didn't let it slip that Frank was a priest. I had to keep my promise to Mom about that.

Nit and I were going to the hospital later to read to Sister Josephine. Maybe Aurora could meet us there too, and we could put our heads together.

Aurora's phone was busy when I called her, but Nit picked up right away.

"Nit, hi, it's me! I was just calling about tonight. Let's go a little early, okay? Maybe six-thirty instead of seven? And I'm going to call Aurora and see if she can go with us. The three of us need to talk!"

"Oh, uh, okay—six-thirty? Well, I'll just meet you out front. You don't need to come in."

"Is everything okay? You sound funny, Nit."

"Yeah, but I gotta go. See you then. Don't forget your rosary this time."

I hung up and redialed Aurora's house. It wasn't busy now, but it took a while for someone to pick up. And when someone did, they didn't say anything.

"H'lo! H'lo! Is anyone there?" I asked.

Someone was breathing heavy into the phone, not saying a word.

"Excuse me," I said in my most official voice. "Is this the Triboni residence?"

The breathing got heavier, and even closer sounding. It was giving me the willies.

"Chip, is that you?" I said. "That's not very polite. Would you please get your sister for me?"

Nothing but raspy, heavy breath back at me.

Chapter 24

I chewed the underside of my lip. I had dialed the right number. I'm very careful about things like that. I hoped everything was okay and that the Tribonis weren't being robbed or anything. I shuddered. Crooks on the brain.

"WhoEVER this is, please put Aurora Triboni on the phone right now, or I'll call the police!"

I heard some yelling in the background. "Bradley! What are you doing with the phone! Did you answer it? You know you're not supposed to."

"Hello!" came a voice over the receiver. "Is someone there?"

"Mrs. Triboni!" I said with relief. "It's Effeline Maloney. May I please speak to Aurora?"

"AUR-O-RA! PHOOONNNE!" she screamed, and then left.

Bradley picked up the phone and continued his breathing.

"You really need to go blow your nose, Bradley," I said, passing the time. "You're all stuffed up. Tell Aurora to get you a Kleenex when she comes."

"Hi, Effie!" Aurora said, coming on the line at last.

"Bradley needs to blow his nose."

"You called to tell me that?"

"No, of course not! I called to ask you if you could meet me and Nit at the hospital tonight with Sister Josephine. You know, it's part of my punishment from Sister Emmanuel. But the reason I really want you to come is so the three of us can talk about something very private."

"Oh, sorry, Ef. I've got basketball practice."

"It's superimportant!" I said.

"How about tomorrow?" she said. "I can meet you right after school."

"Please, Aurora? It's urgent."

"They're counting on me, Effie. I can't just skip."

I sighed hard into the phone.

"Effie, are you okay? Has something bad happened?"

"Of course something has happened! That's why it's urgent. There is something very fishy happening with the man that is living with us. I need to get to the bottom of it, and fast."

"I bet Nit can help you figure something out. She's so smart, Effie. Look, I really gotta hang up. Mom says I have to do the dishes and fold the laundry before she'll let me go. Call me later and give me all the details, okay? Bye now!"

And with that, she hung up on me. Not even waiting for

me to say "bye." Aurora was slipping away faster than I could hold on.

• • •

I asked Frank if he would drive Nit and me to the hospital, which made him very happy. He said he would love to meet her, and maybe on the way home we could all stop and have ice cream.

Trying to sweeten us up.

Mom looked surprised about the whole thing since she knew I wasn't crazy about Frank. So she wouldn't be too suspicious, I told her that I thought she needed to have some alone time with Maxey. You know, to maybe try to shake some sense into her, or give her a reverse exorcism—instead of getting the demons out, we wanted the regular ones we already knew to come back. At least we were used to them.

I called Nit before we left the house to let her know we were on the way, and warned her that Frank would be driving us. I told her I needed her to check him out for me. I wanted her to run him through the special radar she had with people.

Nit wasn't standing alone outside when we got to her house. Though she was trying to be. She looked like she was shoving somebody back into the house when we pulled up.

I climbed out of the car and ran up the steps to her door.

"How are ye!" Donal said, squeezing back out onto the porch when he saw me.

Even in the dark, I could see Nit was embarrassed.

"Donal, what are *you* doing here?" I asked.

"Your girl here told Mr. Giles she'd give me a hand with my studies. My grades are desperate. Da says I've got to pull my socks up! And she didn't want to be a squealer about it."

133

"Oh!" I said. "You're helping him with his homework."

She nodded. "Sorry, I couldn't really tell you."

"It's okay, but let's go. Well, see you tomorrow, Donal!"

I pulled Nit behind me and had her get into the front seat so she could check out Frank better. I leaned over and whispered to her. "Aurora couldn't come, but we still need to talk, okay?"

I climbed into the backseat and then nearly jumped out of my skin. Someone was already there!

"I'll ride along, then," Donal said, grinning at me. "We've done the work, and there's nothing on the telly."

"Don't you have to go home or something?"

"Nah."

Nit turned in her seat. "His dad doesn't pick him up until nine." Then she leaned across to shake Frank's hand. "Hi, I'm Trinity Finch!"

"Oh, sorry!" I leaned over into the front seat. "And this is Frank, my mother's friend from college. Frank, Trinity is my best friend, but we call her Nit."

"Or HG," Donal piped in.

"HG?" Frank asked.

"Fer 'oly Ghost!" Donal said. "But that's not proper, is it?"

"No, I don't suppose it is," Frank said. He turned in his seat and reached a hand over. "And you're . . . ?"

"I'm Donal, from Wexford County, Ir'land."

"Oh, I love Ireland!" Frank said with a big smile. "I'm glad to meet you both."

"My uncle's name is Frank," Donal said. "He's a Guard, and he loves his shorts, he does."

"He *loves* his shorts?" I asked.

Nit giggled, and Frank explained, "He's a policeman. And apparently loves to drink."

I shook my head at Donal. "You couldn't just say that?"

"I did, you silly bird!" he said, giving me a jab in the shoulder.

• • •

Nit and Donal and Frank gabbed all the way to the hospital, but Frank didn't give any real clues away, like accidentally bless them or call them "my child" like a lot of priests do. He was acting like a regular guy who was just bunking up with us and working in our yard. Nit knew exactly what a labyrinth was because she had been to one in London. Really, the girl was a genius. She said she couldn't wait to come over and try it when it was done. She told me I was going to love it. I looked at her like maybe she had mistaken me for someone else.

When we got to the hospital, Frank and Donal decided they'd go to the cafeteria and pick up some "crisps." They'd come get us in a while.

"Well? What do you think?" I asked as we followed the long hallway toward Sister's room.

"He's really nice," she whispered.

"Well, sure, but what else? Did you get any kind of special vibes from him?"

She shrugged. "Yeah, really nice ones."

"Is that *all*?"

"I dunno, something else. I think he's hiding something. I can feel that, but I don't know what it is. Sometimes it takes me a while to sort those things out."

"I just knew it!"

"Knew what? What's going on?"

"He's up to something," I said. "And it's in my backyard, I think!"

"What is it?"

I steered her into a private corner outside Sister's room, then looked around to make sure no one was watching. I pulled the chain around my neck from under my shirt and showed her the key I'd taken from Frank's room. I'd started wearing it so Maxey wouldn't find it and squeal on me.

Nit let out a low whistle. "Wow! Is that a real ruby? Where did you get this?"

"I took it from Frank's room."

"Please tell me you didn't."

"I did! I had to. Something is going on and I have to figure it out. You've got to help me, Nit!"

"We took an oath in Angel Scouts not to steal."

"I know, and I wouldn't steal it. I don't want to keep it. That's a felony, you know. I'm not stupid! I just need to borrow it until I find out what it's for—or at least until Frank finds out it's missing and starts asking about it. That will tell me a lot. He's either going to have a major freak-out about it, and then I'll know the key is to something he shouldn't have. Or he'll just be curious about it, like 'I wonder where I put my gym-locker key.' "

"Let me see it again," she said.

One of the nurse's aides came over and needed the cart we were blocking, so we moved down closer to Sister's room. I looked around again to make sure no one was lurking about, and pulled it out.

Nit turned the key over and over in her hand. "If this is a

gym key, it's to the Queen's gym in Westminster, or maybe even the Pope's gym at the Vatican. It looks religious. Look"—she held it up—"see how it looks like a cross?"

"I know! It could be to some kind of church treasure box he stole. Maybe swiped it from his monsignor. The guy keeps calling Frank—" I said, then stopped.

Nit cocked her head at me. "His monsignor is calling?"

I took a big breath and tried to sound casual. "Oh, yeah, well, I think Frank mentioned he was on some kind of bowling team with a bunch of guys from his church. The monsignor, too, and they're all pretty good friends. So if he did steal something from the church—and I'm not sure that's what he did—it's just because he's around the church a lot and stuff."

I grabbed the key and tucked it back in my shirt, then checked all the buttons on my shirt to make sure it wasn't poking out. Anything to keep from looking at her so I wouldn't blush and give myself away.

"Huh" was all she said for a moment. "So what are you going to do if he doesn't ask after it? Just put it back?"

"No! I need to find out what he's hidden. You and Aurora have to help me find it so we can convince him to give it back. Then he has to leave our house and stay away from my mother forever."

"And if he won't do it?"

"Then I call the police," I said. "But he will, I'm sure of it."

"I don't know, Effie, he seems really, you know, *nice*."

"My dad was nice too," I said. "And look at what he did to our family."

Nit stared right into me. I tried to tear my eyes away, but now I couldn't.

"Okay," I confessed, "I made that part up about the monsignor's bowling league. Sorry! But I can't say any more about that because of a promise I made to my mom."

She seemed to consider that. Finally, she said, "Okay, I'm in. What do you need me to do?"

"Girls!" A shrill voice came from Sister's room. "I've got a broken hip. I'm not deaf. I can hear you out there!"

We ducked in. "Sorry, Sister Josephine," we chorused.

She was sitting propped up in bed, her eyes blind but bright. She was the oldest human being I'd ever seen. She had her rosary threaded through her fingers and her Bible next to her. I'd half expected her to die last time we came. I think we read nearly the entire Old Testament to her. I noticed now and then that Nit wasn't even looking at the page when she was reading. The girl had some of it memorized!

"Well, did you bring it?" Sister asked, looking excited.

Nit unzipped her backpack and pulled out a library book. Sister Josephine reached for it, then ran her hands over the cover with a look of joy. "Is it *Rustlers of West Fork*?"

"Yes, Sister," Nit said.

"Oh," she said with an ache in her voice. "Nobody can write a fight scene like Louis L'Amour."

Nit and I slipped each other a smile.

She clapped her hands. "We're burning daylight, girls. Let's move 'em out!"

Chapter 25

After school on Friday, instead of going to Angel Scouts like we usually did, Nit and I went to Sister's office to pick up Bear for his weekly walk. We knocked, but there was music playing in there, and she didn't hear us. I poked my head in the door.

Some lady in blue jeans and a fringed vest was standing next to the desk going through Sister's private papers. She'd even put a dusty-looking cowboy hat down on Sister's chair. She was going to be in big trouble!

"Excuse me!" I said when she looked up and saw me. "Do you know where Sister Emmanuel is?"

"Come in, girls," she said, turning down her radio.

Nit sidled up next to me and gasped. "Is that you, Sister?"

The woman clipped a leash onto Bear's collar. He gave her a fussy growl.

"Now, Bear!" she said. "I don't want any nonsense from you."

I drew in my breath. It was her!

She came up to us then, handing him over. "Well, go ahead. You might as well get a full look!"

"You look—you look . . . ," I stammered.

"Great!" Nit exclaimed, giving me a sneaky elbow jab.

"Thank you, Trinity. Since you must be wondering, I might as well tell you. I ride with the rodeos on the weekend. Brings in a little extra income for the convent, and I enjoy it."

"Do all the Sisters have weekend jobs?" I asked, trying to absorb this.

She almost, but not quite, smiled at that. "No, just me." She reached into her top drawer and pulled out a doggy treat for Bear. He swallowed it whole like a pill and wagged his tail for more.

"I heard you used to be a champion barrel racer," I said. "Did you give it up so you could be a nun?"

"I still compete. Not as much. But I really love it, and Mother Superior has been kind enough to let me continue with it—just on the weekends, of course."

"Do you miss being a full-time cowgirl?"

She handed Bear's leash over to me. "Sometimes in life, girls, you have to make hard choices. You follow your heart, and mine led me here."

"We won't tell anyone we saw you in pants," Nit said. "You can count on us."

"Thank you, Trinity, but it doesn't really matter." She

picked up her hat and her keys. "Might be a nice change to have something true going around school for a change. Over the years the children have told lots of stories about me—the latest I heard was that I'm a vampire!"

That was courtesy of Aurora, I bet. I didn't dare tell Sister there was another rumor that she went on a secret Valentine's Day date.

"C'mon, boy," I said when Sister handed Bear's leash to me.

She reached into her pocket and pulled out a big stopwatch. "When you're done, you can leave him with Sister Lucille at the convent. I want you girls to take him on a nice long walk tonight. I've spoken with Mrs. Finch, and she said she'll pick you up after she gets off work at six."

She handed us a couple of plastic bags. "And make sure he does his business before you bring him back. He had a big bowl of stew for lunch, so he'll be anxious to go, I'm sure."

"Yes, Sister." I tried not to gag.

When we got in front of the school, I steered him to the left and we took off.

"We've got an hour and fifteen minutes before . . ." I said, trailing off but giving Nit a pointed look.

"Oh! We're going to Sam Houston's?"

I smiled. "You read my mind. Think we can make it over there and back in time?"

"We can try!" Nit said. "It's not too far, is it?"

"I don't think so. She's got practice tonight, so I know she'll be there."

"Did you tell her we were going to come?"

"No, I wanted to surprise her. We've all got so much to

talk about! The party is just one week away. I mailed Aurora's invitation to her. She really liked it. And I've gotten RSVPs from everyone at school. They're all coming!"

"And don't forget, we need to tell her about Kayla!" Nit said.

"Not until after the party! If she knew that Kayla was the one who hired the choir to sing and everything, she'd be so mad she might not want to come."

"I guess you're right about that," Nit said. "Man, I can't wait until we go to camp. We are going to get her and get her good!"

Bear stopped to scarf down a half-eaten apple on the sidewalk. Then he wanted to sit down and rest. I tugged on his leash. "Upsy-daisy!" I said. "Help me pull, Nit."

We hurried him along as best we could, but he wanted to stop and sniff every tree and leave his personal autograph with it. Every now and then, Nit would have to get behind him and lift him up by the haunches. "He weighs a ton!" she said, huffing. "I think we're getting more exercise than he is."

"Do you think we're getting close?" I asked after a while. "I don't remember it being this far down."

"I dunno," she said.

A cold wind whipped through our skirts, making them fly up. I kept batting mine down and wished I'd changed into pants. "Is it getting dark already?" I looked up at the sky.

"It's just really black clouds."

We were in a neighborhood now where we didn't know any of the kids. I started getting a creepy feeling, like maybe we were being watched, even followed. I could tell Nit was sensing it too. Normally we wouldn't be so spooked, because we'd have Aurora with us. She wasn't afraid of anything. But on our own, it felt different.

"Let's put our Angel Scout beanies back on," I said, reaching into my backpack. "Just in case anyone wants to mess with us, they'll know they're not just messing with us, but with the Big Guy in the Sky too."

"Let's not. They look stupid," Nit said. "I hate those flappy wings on the top. And it might make things worse. We've already got our uniforms on. They're pretty hard to miss."

"Just put it on, will you?" I said.

She grumbled as she went through her pack to get it out.

I kept hearing something behind us, but I couldn't see anything. Nit and I walked closer together against the wind and tried to get Bear to move faster. A strange hooting sound started near us. Made us both jump.

"An owl," Nit said. "Sounds big and nasty, doesn't it?"

Bear didn't even seem to hear it. The only thing he was watching for was more snacks on the sidewalk. Nit pulled her big cross out from under her jacket and put it on the outside. "Just in case, you know."

I didn't think we were being followed by a hooting vampire, but you could just never be too sure what a gang of public-school kids might do, I thought. And we were on their turf now.

The hair on the back of my neck started to bristle, and I looked behind me again. This time I thought I saw something or someone dart behind a tree. My heart sped up, and I picked up the pace.

Just then, a terrible roaring noise came from right behind us.

"*RUN, BEAR!*" I yelled.

We ran the next two blocks as fast as we could, hanging on to our beanies and yelling at Bear to keep moving. Our backpacks flopped up and down.

The roaring continued. "*Faster, Nit, hurry!*" I screamed.

Feet pounded behind us, closer and closer.

We raced into the school parking lot, heading for the lit-up basketball courts.

"There's Aurora!" I grabbed Nit's shirt and pulled her with me.

Bear growled and began to bark, finally, snapping his big jaws.

We raced onto the court and threw ourselves at Aurora just as she was jumping for a shot.

Bear ran in wild circles around us, wrapping us up in his leash.

The kids yelled and hooted.

"FOUL!"

"That's NOT a foul! They're not in the game!"

"Nice HATS, girls!"

"GET THAT DOG OFF THE COURT!"

"Effie! Nit!" Aurora yelled. "*BEAR!* What are you guys doing here?"

I tried to talk, my chest heaving. "They're chasing us!" I whipped my head in all directions, looking for them.

"Nit!" I cried. "Where'd they all go?"

She was trying to catch her breath and untangle us from the leash.

"*Who* was chasing you?" Aurora asked.

"You wanna play or what, Triboni! Get your little friends off the court NOW!"

A dark figure wearing a hoodie all zipped up sidled over. Aurora grabbed it and yanked the hood back.

Donal gave her a silly grin. "Hey, oul' girl! Been bloody ages!"

Chapter 26

"YOU!" I yelled. "You about scared us to death!"

"Donal!" Nit said. "What the heck are you doing?"

Aurora pulled him off the court by the hood. He laughed as he went.

"TRIBONI!" A girl even bigger than Fancy yelled. "You gonna play ball or WHAT!"

"In a minute!" she called over her shoulder.

"She'll be right back," I offered helpfully to the big girl.

"Who the hell are you?"

"I'm Effie, and this is Nit. And this is Bear." He looked up, drooling. "We go to St. Dominic's, and we're Aurora's best friends. And that—" I said, pointing over to Donal.

"Get off the court NOW," she said, with bad onion breath.

Fancy came storming over. "Triboni! You want to play ball

or you gonna have a prayer meeting with your little friends here?"

"I'm in!" Aurora said. She stabbed Donal in the chest with her finger. "You don't mess with my friends—you hear me?"

"I was having a bit of a game! Sorry!"

Fancy spit on the ground next to us. "I sure hate to interrupt your St. Dumb-i-nics class reunion, Triboni! You about done?"

"Yeah, sorry," Aurora said. "I can't talk now, you guys. I gotta go."

"That's okay!" Nit said. "We'll wait until you're done."

"But I can't talk then, either," she said. "The team is going out for pizza. I didn't know you were coming!"

She jumped back into the game. "Call me tomorrow!" she yelled.

Nit and I stared at each other.

Donal came up next to us. "Got the fifty?"

"Fifty what?" I shot at him, peeved.

"Stood up," Nit said. " 'Got the fifty' means we got stood up."

"We did *not*! She's just very busy," I hissed.

Donal zipped his hoodie back up and pulled it over his head. "Righto."

"She's not dumping us!" I yelled as he slunk back into the night.

And those were my last words before the basketball came flying toward me and hit me smack dead center in the face.

• • •

"You don't think she did it on purpose, do you?" Nit asked me as we sat in front of Sam Houston's waiting for Mrs.

Finch to come pick us up. I moved the wad of ice in a napkin from my mouth. It was swelling. Aurora had given me the ice out of her soda, and we put it in a napkin.

"Who, Fancy? I dunno," I said. I wiped my nose with my sleeve. At least that had stopped bleeding. "How's my lip look?"

"Big. Does it still hurt?"

Bear lay on his side next to us, snoring in a dead sleep. He'd seen a lot of action in the last hour, and he was worn out.

"It's okay," I said, touching it with my finger and then wincing. "I can't believe Aurora would rather have pizza with mean sixth graders instead of being with us."

"Yeah, I know," Nit said. "She sort of acted like she was embarrassed of us."

"Us?" I said. "She's the one who should be embarrassed. Her team wasn't very nice at all. And we'd walked all the way over there to surprise her and everything."

"I know, Ef. I'm just saying."

Nit handed me her water bottle and I took a tiny sip, but I couldn't feel my lips, and it dribbled onto my jacket. When I wiped it off, my lip started to bleed again.

Nit handed me the ice pack back. "Keep this on longer."

"We've got to get her back to St. Dom's," I said. "They'll ruin her. We should have never let her go in the first place," I said.

"Effie, she wanted to come here, that was obvious. It's not just about getting away from Marcus. Here, she's the hotshot fourth grader that plays on the sixth-grade team."

"I know, but *we're* not here!"

"We can't make her come back unless she wants to."

"I know," I said, sighing. "Everything was going so well and now look at the mess we have!"

"It will all work out, Ef." She gave me a squeeze around the shoulders.

"Nit, what are we going to do about Frank and the loot? We didn't even get a chance to talk to Aurora about it tonight."

"First off, we can't jump to conclusions."

"I'm not jumping, I'm deducing—he's up to no good in my backyard. He might as well have put up a flashing sign that says 'X marks the spot'!"

. . .

Nit was still looking at me like I'd gone crazy by the time Mrs. Finch came and picked us up. She noticed my very swollen, bloody mouth right off and called my mother to warn her. She threw away my bloody napkins and gave me some clean ones. She spent most all the way home muttering and clucking over the public-school hooligans and checking on me in her rearview mirror to make sure I wasn't spurting blood all over her car. Or that Bear wasn't eating her upholstery.

He wasn't, but he was sharing some stinky effects of his stew. We all rolled down the windows and tried to breathe. Mrs. Finch, who was a glamorous makeup lady at Dillard's department store, looked like she was ready to ditch the car and the whole lot of us.

I leaned back in the seat and tried to cover my nose, which was really sore. I could tell that Nit hadn't entirely bought my theory about Frank. It was kind of hard to explain the whole thing without mentioning that he was a priest.

When we pulled in front of my house, I thanked Mrs. Finch.

Nit leaned over the seat and whispered into my ear, "Does this Frank thing mean we're going to have to dig up your whole backyard?"

I whispered back, "Just the part where the treasure is."

"That's a relief."

I think she was being sarcastic, but I couldn't tell because it was too dark.

I hurried up the walk as fast as I could because I knew Mrs. Finch would wait until I was safely in. I leaned on the door to shove it open with my shoulder, but Frank pulled it open.

"Whoa!" he said.

"You're always right—right—*there!*" I snapped, then brushed past him and headed upstairs.

"I'm sorry, Effie."

Not as sorry as I was.

Chapter 27

Mom was just coming down with her giant coach's first-aid kit. She didn't hear my snarky remark to Frank.

"There you are! Let's take a look at that mouth." She is pretty much an expert at faces that get smashed by flying basketballs. Happens all the time at her job.

She herded me to the upstairs bathroom and had me hop up on the sink.

"Do any of your teeth feel loose?"

"Uh-uh."

"Bet it hurts, huh?" She went to work with Q-tips and cotton balls.

"Yesh."

"How'd you manage to take a ball in the face? Did you get

in the game?" She handed me a tissue. "Blow your nose. And what were you doing at Sam Houston's?"

I shook my head. Blew. Even that hurt. "We were just trying to take Bear for a good long walk, and we wanted to go to Aurora's practice. I wasn't even on the court! This mean girl named Fancy threw it out of bounds, and I got smashed. She might have done it on purpose."

Mom stopped her poking and looked at me. "That was too far for you girls to be walking without permission, and you know that, miss. We'll deal with that later. Now, tell me why some girl would want to hit you in the face."

I sighed. "She didn't like us talking to Aurora and stuff during practice." I started to tell Mom about crashing onto the court after Donal chased us, but I decided I better not.

"What did Aurora think about Fancy doing that?" she asked. "Did she get mad at her?"

I lifted my shoulders, then dropped them. "She didn't really see it. She was guarding somebody. She felt bad when she saw I was bleeding, but you know, she had to get back to the game. She did pour all her soda out and give me her ice. She really wants to play with the sixth graders."

"Well, that's a pretty big deal for a fourth-grade girl."

Mom finished her work and started putting away her things. "Good as new!" she said. "I can't say the same for your shirt, though."

I looked down at the blood drops all over the front of my good school blouse. "Sorry."

"Don't worry about it," she said, tweaking my ear, about the only thing on my face that didn't hurt.

"I think I'm losing my best friend to basketball."

She leaned up against the counter. "Yeah?"

"I guess Nit and I thought that Aurora would hate public school so much she'd want to come back and everything would work out. I think she loves it! Plus, Nit thinks it's easier for her to be tall and have boobs and hair in private places at public school. Do you think that's true?"

"Maybe," Mom said. "Sam Houston's has a lot more kids in general, all kinds of them. She probably doesn't feel she stands out as much there."

I considered that. And then, "Would you let me go to public school, Mom?"

She raised her eyebrows. "What about Nit? Did you forget you have two best friends?"

I licked my lip. I didn't want to leave Nit, of course. "Maybe her mom would let her go, too."

"Do you really want to go to another school, or do you just want to be with Aurora?"

"I want the three of us to all be together again."

"I know, cupcake. But that's not a very good reason to change schools. Maybe you can figure something else out."

"Like what?"

She tapped me gently on the forehead. "I'll leave that to you and this very fine brain of yours."

The bathroom door swung open and Maxey stepped in. I turned so she couldn't see my face.

"What happened?" she asked, seeing the first-aid kit and bloody tissues on the counter. She gasped. "You didn't start your period did you?" she nearly screamed. "You better not have before me!"

"No!" I hollered. "Go away!"

"Were you picking your nose, Effie? I've told her, Mom . . ."

"Of course she wasn't," Mom said. "She got hit in the face with a ball."

"Leave," I said. "You didn't even knock, either."

Maxey turned on her heel and left, closing the door behind her.

Mom smiled at me. "Will wonders never cease?"

There was a soft knock on the door.

I sighed.

"Effie!" Mom said. "She's trying. Be nice."

Boy, if this wasn't a world turned upside down. Maxey was doing what I asked her to do, and Mom telling *me* to be nice!

"Come *in*!" I said, hopping off the sink.

She peered around the door. "I just wanted to ask you two if there is anything special you need some prayers for."

Mom gave Maxey a squeeze around the shoulders. "I'll take a victory over the Tigers this weekend. They're undefeated. Effie, how about you?"

I folded my arms across my chest. "World peace, lady priests, straight hair, a new car, and for Frank to go back to his church."

• • •

I called Aurora early the next day because I knew she didn't have practice, and it was her morning to be home to watch Bradley. As usual, he picked up the phone and started the heavy-breathing routine.

I cut to the chase. "Bradley, it's Effie. If you go get Aurora for me right now, I'll bring you a *big* cookie next time I come over."

"Cook-ie?" he said.

"Yes, now go get her!"

Fourteen minutes later, Aurora finally picked up the phone. "Anyone there?"

"Thank God! It's me! Geez, what took so long?"

"Well, Bradley kept yelling about cookies. We don't have any in the house right now, but I couldn't convince him. He started bawling, so I had to make some frosting real quick and put it on a piece of bread to settle him down."

"Yuck!" I said. "And sorry about that. I told him I'd give him a cookie next time I came over if he went and got you."

"Well, no wonder, Ef. He's just a little kid. He doesn't understand *future* cookies. He only understands *now* cookies. Anyway, how are you, and how's your lip? I feel so bad about you getting smacked in the face!"

"It's okay," I said, touching it.

"I wish you guys would have told me you were coming!"

"We just wanted to surprise you," I said. "We really needed to talk to you—well, I really needed to talk to you. It's about Frank, my mother's friend that's staying with us."

"So what's up with that?"

"I can't really talk right now, in case someone might be listening, but can you come over for dinner tonight? Nit is coming. We really need to do some planning for the slumber party. Only one more week! And I can't wait."

"I think I can come, I just need to double-check. But about your party, Ef . . ."

"It's not really my party, Aurora, it's *our* party—yours, mine, Nit's."

"Right—well, you see, I might not exactly be able to come to it, after all."

"*WHAAAAT?*"

"I know, I'm so sorry! It's not for sure, but it's Fancy's birthday next weekend, and she's invited the whole team to a big party. Her mom is going to drive us all to Houston to go ice-skating. She says they have this new outdoor rink that is totally slick."

"But, Aurora, it's all planned, and you already said you were coming!"

"I know, Effie, and I feel like a big wart about it, but it's my *team*. Everyone has to be there. If I didn't go, Fancy would be really mad. She might even kick me off."

Like that would be bad?

She went on, "Is there any way that you could move your party to another night?"

"No! I've already sent out the invitations. And everyone is coming!" This was terrible. I couldn't believe it. "Well, could you at least come for the sleepover part? You know, when you get back from Houston, could Fancy's mom bring you over here?"

Aurora was quiet a minute and then said, "Well, Fancy wants me to have a sleepover with her afterward."

This just kept getting worse. "All the team? Or just you."

She cleared her throat, then said in a small voice, "Just me."

"But you said no, right?" Please, Aurora, tell me you said no.

"I haven't exactly said no yet. I wanted to talk to you first. I hate to say no to her, Ef. She's kind of lonely, and I didn't want to hurt her feelings. Plus, it's her birthday and all. I mean, if it was your birthday, I wouldn't even think about going to her house."

Kind of lonely? Oh, no, she was trying to get Aurora to be her new best friend!

"Effie, how about this? You have your very fun, cool party, and I'll go to my party with my team, and I'll do the sleepover with Fancy just to be polite. But then next weekend, you and Nit can come over here for a sleepover. We can do all the same games and everything! That would be almost as good, wouldn't it?"

I felt like I was going to cry, but I didn't want to do that in front of her.

"Effie, are you still there? Please don't be sore at me."

"I'm not," I said, my voice a tight knot. "But I need to go. My mom is waving at me to come help her in the kitchen."

"What about dinner tonight?" she asked. "What time should I come?"

"Oh, gosh, did I say dinner *tonight*? I meant next week. I'm getting things so confused with all the party planning and shopping. Sorry! I'll talk to you later! Bye!"

I clicked the phone off. As much as I had wanted her to come over, I was not in the mood to be an understanding best friend. I watched the picture in my head of my party as it burst into flame and went right up in smoke. Bright green St. Patrick's Day smoke. Where the heck had all my good luck gone?

I grabbed a black Magic Marker from the drawer under the phone and went over to my list of lucky things.

Slashed a line right through number eight. My good luck had just gone south.

Chapter 28

Even though I'm really too old to still climb trees, after I talked to Aurora, my nearly ex–best friend, I went out back and shimmied up our old maple tree. It has a perfect sitting perch near the top. Maxey fell out of it once and broke her arm, so she stopped climbing it. It's the one place at our house that I can always have all to myself. When I was in first grade, I told Mom that I wanted to get married up in my tree, and I was going to decorate it with hundreds of twinkling lights. All the guests could stand under the tree, but me and my boyfriend and the priest would climb up. I already had our branches picked out.

I wrapped my arms around a big familiar branch and rested my head. Even though nobody could see me now, I still didn't want to cry. Crying always made me feel worse, not better, like some people said it would. Principal Obermeyer once told me that crying never makes her feel better either. I wished she'd come back from her stupid sabbatical. I bet none of this would have happened if she'd been here.

The back door opened and Frank came out. Oh, rats. If I stayed very still, he probably wouldn't even know I was up here. That suited me fine. But I had nothing against spying on him awhile.

He walked out into the middle of the yard and unfolded his labyrinth plans from his back pocket. Then he took the pencil out from behind his ear and made some notes on his paper. I wished I could get a better view of it. Maybe he had marked the spot where he had buried his loot, if he had buried it yet.

He had about half the stepping-stones laid already, and just yesterday, he'd brought home a truckload of river pebbles and tons of new things to plant. Some even big and fully grown. I heard Mom tell him that it must be costing him a fortune, and he told her not to worry, as it was the least he could do for us. He was also going to make a little pond, with some real fish and a tiny waterfall, but that wouldn't be until after my party. Maxey told me she heard him even trying to convince Mom to let him put in a hot tub out back for us. But supposedly she put her foot down and said that was just too extravagant for us. What would the town think?

Frank went and sat down on one of the big flat labyrinth stones and pulled his knees up to his chin. He just sat there hugging his legs for a while. From up here he looked like such a regular guy, even like he might be a nice one to have around. I always felt a little jealous of kids who had dads who worked in the yard and remembered to get the oil changed in the car before it started smoking like ours did.

A feeling I didn't like shot through me just then—a mix of pure sadness, envy, and wishing. I was coveting all the things my neighbors had, like the Ten Commandments say you're not supposed to do. I wasn't coveting the neighbor's wife, of course. I didn't need one of those. I was sad that I didn't have a dad I could count on, and I was jealous that so many other kids did.

And I wished that my mom wasn't a crook magnet. Why did Frank have to come here, and why did she let him stay? Wasn't she happy with just the three of us anymore?

I had to figure out how to help her, but I felt very alone. And, honestly, I hated to think about what this would do to Maxey when she found out.

"So, how does it look from up there?" Frank asked in a quiet voice, without turning around.

Dang it. I didn't say anything for a second. And then, "How does what look?" I snapped.

"The labyrinth."

"Looks okay."

"Can I come up and see?" he asked.

"There's no room for you."

"Okay," he said, cheerful. "You tell me what it looks like, then."

Oh, for Pete's sake. Would he ever stop trying to make friends with me?

"It looks okay."

"I can't wait until it's done!"

"What are you going to do with that one giant hole over there?" I asked.

"I think that would be a good place to put the small pond. What do you think?"

"I don't care one way or the other."

He was quiet after that. Finally. But then I started thinking that since we were alone and he seemed to be so crazy mad to talk to me, maybe I should see what I could learn.

So, as innocent as I could, like maybe I was just sitting up the tree, missing my father like some pitiful kid, I asked, "You knew my dad, right?"

"Not too well, Ef."

"But you met him, right?"

"Yes, he and your mom came to my ordination."

"What do priests do if they need to go to confession?" I asked, changing the subject quick, like the TV cops do to throw a guy off.

"We go to a priest," he said. "Same as you."

"But you go to a different town so they don't recognize you, right?"

"No," he chuckled. "But that's not a bad idea."

"Have you been to confession since you've been staying with us?"

"No," he said. "Do you think I should go?"

"I don't know. Do you have something you need to confess?"

He didn't say anything for a minute. "Yeah, I do, Effie. Would you hear my confession?"

"Me? I'm not a priest, I can't. You know that."

"Well, you can't officially, in the sacramental way. But you are my sister in Christ, and I would be honored if you'd hear my unofficial confession. Confessing our faults and short-comings to one another is a very healing process."

Was he kidding me? "Do you mean it?"

"Really!"

I was out of that tree faster than a squirrel to an acorn festival. I jumped the last four feet and nearly knocked him over.

"Where do you want me?" I asked.

"How about right there?" he said, pointing to the next labyrinth stone over.

I dropped down and crossed my legs. "Do you want me to close my eyes or anything?"

"Only if you want to." He made the Sign of the Cross, so I made one too.

I was all ears.

Chapter 29

"I haven't been exactly straight with your mom," he confessed.

I knew it! "Was your ordination a fake?"

"No," he said, looking at me, surprised. "I'm really a priest, Effie."

"You never go to Mass."

"I know. It's difficult for me to be there right now. I know that must be confusing for you."

"Then what are you lying to my mom about?"

"Well, I haven't said anything to her that was untrue, but I did lead her to believe that I needed a place to stay. I've allowed her to go on thinking something that isn't entirely true."

I waited, and when he didn't say anything, I had to ask. "What isn't true?"

"I didn't really *need* a place to stay. I just mean that I have more money than I'll ever be able to spend. I could stay anywhere. I just really wanted to stay here with all of you."

"Maybe you should pay us rent, then," I said.

He smiled. "I'd love to, but she won't let me. So this labyrinth," he said, motioning around us, "is one way I'm trying to earn my keep. I guess I was afraid of just asking if I could stay. I didn't think she'd understand. I'm not sure I even understand it myself. I didn't come here that Sunday morning with the intention of moving in. I was missing your mom something fierce, and after I saw you all, I really wanted to be a part of your home for a while. And when I saw your backyard, and the state it was in, it captured me. I wanted to make a beautiful place for all of you. And I love working out here. It's so peaceful, and everything makes sense out here."

"This is kind of a confusing confession, Frank. And how come you're rolling in the dough if you're a priest? Is it all from your uncle Ruben, or did the Pope give you guys a big raise or something?" Not that I believed that for a second, but I wanted to see if I could catch him up in his own lies.

At that, he threw back his head and laughed. "No raises from the Pope, I'm afraid. I've made some investments that have paid off quite nicely. I don't get much of a chance to spend it, though. I'd love to go out and buy your mom a new car, but she'd hit the ceiling."

And, then, right for the jugular. "How long have you been in love with my mother?"

"Are you asking me as my confessor?"

"Yes," I said, folding my arms over my chest and trying to look official.

"Then I confess," he said. "I've always loved your mother. And there was a time long ago that I was very much *in* love with her. But God decided to fill up my dance card instead."

"Is she in love with you?"

"Her heart is full to the brim with you and Maxey."

I looked at him.

"Effie, I'm not here to steal your mother away, or to try to take anyone's place."

"Maxey thinks you don't want to be a priest anymore and that's why you're here."

He sighed and picked up a small stone. Rubbed it on his pant leg. "Some days I honestly don't."

"Why not? It seems like a pretty good job for you." I almost said "cover" instead of "job" but caught myself in time.

"I love serving the people—especially those who are overlooked in the world. I don't much enjoy the business part of the Church, though I know it's needed. And I don't always agree with the Church, though I love it." He looked at me and tossed me the pebble. "Sort of like you love Maxey, but she drives you a little crazy sometimes."

"Yeah, but you get to move out or stop being a priest if you want. I'm stuck with her. I wish you'd turn her back to the way she was."

"What do you mean?"

"You know, stop turning her into a holy nutcase."

"All I've really done is try to set a good example and help her with her religion class. I think what you're seeing is Maxey trying very hard to be perfect—" He stopped a moment.

"So are you going to just split when you're done here?" I butted in.

"There you are, Frank!" Maxey called from the back door. "I finished my religion homework," she said. "Can you come check it?"

"Be right there, Max."

He turned back toward me. "So that's my confession. Thanks for hearing me out. I've been feeling like a chump about it."

"You need to tell Mom you have a lot of money and don't need a place to stay." And I hope you leave today, I thought.

He gave one of my boingy curls a tweak as he unfolded his legs. "You're right, Effie. False pretenses are never right. I'll tell her right away."

"Hold on!" I said. "For your penance, say thirty Hail Marys, umm, donate a thousand dollars to St. Dominic's—we need better hoops at my school, and some of those big outdoor lights so you can play ball at night, and . . ." I searched my mind for one last thing. "Oh! And empty Pretty Girl's litter box for a week."

"Done!" He gave me a thumbs-up and jogged back to the house.

I stayed sitting for a while longer and tried to sort out all I'd just learned. He was already loaded. So maybe he'd been a crook for a while, and this wasn't his first job. Or maybe he was making up that part to throw me off. Maybe he knew I was on to him.

I wasn't too sure about whether he still had the hots for my mom. And he definitely did not answer the question about whether my mom was in love with him.

And then, the most important question of all—what was in our backyard? Was there a treasure buried out here? And, if so, who buried it—my dad or Frank? I just had to bring Nit here. She was so good at finding things.

Mom was so excited about it. She kept saying she couldn't wait to use it. I did not want to get in big trouble for messing it up.

My plate was seriously running-eth over.

• • •

There was a very bad smell in my house when I went back inside, and a scary sight to go with it. Maxey had taken over the dining-room table and had set up some kind of home beauty shop. She was mixing up a nasty brew in what happened to be my favorite cereal bowl. Of course.

"What are you doing?" I asked.

"Giving Mom highlights," she said with a huge grin.

"No, you're not."

"I am too," she said, squeezing another dollop of something smelly into the bowl. Then she stirred it up. "It's my reward for bringing my religion grade up," she smugged.

"Does she know about this?" I couldn't believe Mom would go for this.

"Of course!" she said. "Like I could sneak them on her head."

"Well, where is she then?"

"She went upstairs to put on an old shirt, but she'll be right back. Frank went out for a run, so it's the perfect time."

"I bet Mom climbed out the upstairs window," I said,

shaking my head. "Maxey, do you even know *how* to do highlights?"

"*Yeess!*"

"Where'd you learn?" I said, moving closer to sniff.

"I watched someone do it once. And I called over to Salon Sensation and talked to some guy about it. He told me how much to mix in. Plus there were instructions that came with it. Don't worry! I'm nearly a professional."

"I like Mom's hair the way it is! Why do you want to go and change it?"

Maxey gave me a look like she was twenty-nine and I was three. "Mom needs to look a little hotter. She looks so coachish, you know?"

"Who does she need to look hot for? She doesn't even have a boyfriend."

"My point exactly."

"Maxey, are you doing this so Frank will fall in love with her?"

She cocked one shoulder up and then pulled on a pair of rubber gloves. "I wouldn't try to tempt him away from the Church," she said, innocent.

"You would if you thought it would keep him here."

She looked around to make sure he hadn't wandered back in. "What would be so wrong with that, anyway? You need a father, Effie. You're turning into a little man-hater. You and your little friends."

"I don't want Father Frank for my father!"

"Well, fine, then think of me for a change, will you? It's not easy being the oldest and having so much responsibility. I need some help here," she said, pointing a spatula at me.

"Plus, I may need some male guidance. My puberty is coming any minute now, and I could go bad. Some girls do."

"Maxey, you already went bad."

She picked up a hand mirror from the table. "Don't you think I'd look hot with highlights?"

Chapter 30

On the day of my first-ever slumber party, Mom let us all have the afternoon off from school so we could get ready for the party. We stopped at the grocery store on the way home and bought all the special nitrate-free pepperoni and other toppings for the pizzas we were going to make. And she let us buy real sodas, not the fake kind that nobody ever heard of. And we bought a lot of green mint chocolate chip ice cream, and green food coloring to put in the whipped cream. I could nearly have fainted from how excited I was. I had barely slept at all the night before, and I sure wasn't going to sleep much that night.

Then we stopped at the party store and bought balloons. With my own allowance, I bought party favors for everyone, and even Maxey pitched in for that too. We were making little gold gift bags with gum, chocolate coins, glitter nail polish, stickers, and some lick-on tattoos.

The only part that was giving me the nervous willies was that Aurora had talked me into letting her bring Fancy to my party, after they got back from theirs. It was either that or she was going to spend the night at Fancy's house. At least this way I'd have her here with all of her old St. Dom's buddies. She'd see how much nicer and more fun we were.

At first I couldn't figure out why Fancy would even agree to it, but Aurora told her my mom was a basketball coach. That sealed the deal for her.

Nit said it was a good compromise. And maybe Fancy would be so tired from ice-skating in Houston and bossing everyone around that she'd fall asleep early. Then me, Aurora, Nit, and all our classmates could have our special time together. Eleven girls were coming, plus Fancy and Aurora, so that made thirteen. I was trying to ignore the fact that thirteen was an unlucky number. But all the green shamrocks we were using to decorate would undo any bad luck hanging around. We hung so many up that it was probably going to be a very lucky night for me!

Frank was putting the finishing touches on the labyrinth and made us all promise that we wouldn't come out to look until he told us he was ready. He'd even gotten up before dawn and made all the green pizza dough, and it was ready in the fridge for us to put the stuff on top. Plus, he made frosted sugar cookies, and he and Mom were going to help me write everyone's name on them with the new frosting shooter that he bought. It had more attachments than our vacuum cleaner. I hoped when he moved out he would forget to take it with him.

Mom sat down with Maxey and me while we were stuffing the party bags. Her cheeks were red and she was a little sweaty from hanging a giant rainbow banner over the staircase. It said WELCOME TO EFFIE'S ST. PATRICK'S SLUMBER BASH! She'd made a few of them on her computer last night after we went to bed. I hadn't been to a slumber party before, so I wasn't too sure if you were supposed to decorate so much, especially since it wasn't my birthday. But I didn't want to hurt her feelings. She was having fun.

"Thanks, Mom!" I said. "Everything looks great!"

Even Mom did, if you could believe it. Maxey had done a pretty good job on Mom's hair. There was just one part in the back that had kind of a highlight clump, but the front looked nice. It had taken a lot longer than Maxey had planned. She used up all the aluminum foil in the house, and Frank had to go out for more. Maxey's arms finally got so tired from holding up Mom's long strands of hair that Frank started helping. He was pretty good at it.

He and Maxey kept joking about opening their own salon and naming it Holy Rollers. Ha-ha. A couple of comedians.

Mom took a big swig of iced mint tea that Frank had made her. She smiled as she looked around. "It does look pretty nice, doesn't it? Do you think we need more streamers?"

Maxey looked and said, "I think you have more than enough put up already. Waste is a sin, you know."

Mom gave her a smack on the bottom. "Don't be a party pooper, Maxey."

Maxey pressed her lips together hard to keep a smart-aleck remark from escaping. Mom peeked into one of the finished bags. Maxey tried to grab it away. "Don't touch it!"

"I'm just looking," Mom said. She reached in and pulled out a card. She turned it around for us to see. It was a holy card with Joan of Arc on it being burned at the stake.

"You're giving out holy cards?" she asked me.

"MAXEY!" I yelled. "Did you put that in there?"

"St. Joan of Arc is a very inspirational role model for girls!" she said.

Mom rubbed her forehead. "Maxey, take them all out. This is Effie's party. You chose not to have one, remember?"

"Oh, fine,". she muttered.

"Is there anything else I should know about?" I said. "You didn't hide a rosary in the cake mix, did you?"

"Don't be silly," she said. "Someone might choke on it."

I looked up at Mom, pleading. "Could you please send her somewhere tonight? Maybe drop her off in a church? I don't trust her."

"She'll be fine. Don't worry," Mom said. "Maxey, would you like to be the first to walk the labyrinth tonight?"

Her face broke out in a huge smile. "Really? You'll let me do it first?"

"*If* you promise, no more shenanigans!"

"Promise!" she said. "I bet the first person to christen a labyrinth gets all their prayers or problems answered."

"Well, I can't guarantee that." Frank came into the room, drying his hands on a dish towel. "But I'm sure that God has a very special blessing for anyone who truly is looking for Him."

"See?" she said, elbowing me.

Which made me knock over Mom's whole glass of iced tea, right on top of the last gold bag I was filling. "Oh, no! Look what you did!" I yelled.

Frank threw down his dish towel and tried to blot it off, but everything was soaked.

"It's ruined! Now we'll be one short," I moaned.

"You'll just have to give up the one that was meant for you," Maxey said. "It's better to give than receive anyway, right, Frank?"

"Can it, Maxey," Mom said. She kept trying to wipe the bag off, but it was no use.

"Well, I've got some good news!" Frank said, trying to lighten things up.

Unless it involved an extra favor bag he had, I didn't give a flip.

"Is it done?" Mom asked.

"It is done!" he said. "The Maloney Labyrinth is now open."

"Hooray!" Maxey said. "Can I go in it now?"

"Let's all go look!" Mom said, prying the sopping wet stickers out of my hands.

"Do I have to, Mom?" I asked. "I'm really busy! And I didn't get to write the names on the cookies yet."

Frank looked like I'd just ridden off on his birthday pony. Mom gave me a secret ouchy pinch on the back of my arm and pushed me out the back door. "There's plenty of time for everything!"

Maxey danced her way out the door and Frank came up behind us. "Kath, don't make her if she doesn't want to. It can wait."

"Don't be silly! This is something to celebrate."

Maxey stood still as a statue at the bottom of the porch steps. We nearly ran into her. Then we stopped, too, and just took it all in. And drew in our breath.

It was like some kind of magic fairyland. Hundreds and

hundreds of tiny white lights sparkled in all the trees, the bushes, and even some new small trees that I'd never seen before. And there were really cool torchlights planted in the ground that wound around with the steps of the labyrinth. I followed Maxey around the maze, backward and forward, then out another side. My mouth was hanging open. It was amazing! I could hardly believe it was our old yard.

I turned at the sound of trickling water that was coming from some kind of fountain nearby. And music! Where was the music coming from?

"What is that?" Maxey asked. She twirled to look at Frank.

"I installed some speakers out here. It's connected to a sound dock in your mom's office. Those are monks chanting. Nice, isn't it? But you can play any kind of music out here. It will be great for you girls when you start having dance parties."

"Did you do all this yourself today?" Mom gasped.

"Well, I hired a few extra hands to help me get it done while you were all out today. And a nice boy down the street came by, and he helped for a while."

"We don't have any nice boys on our street," I said.

"Short kid trying to grow a mustache?" he said.

"A Turner boy?" Maxey and I asked in unison.

"Yeah, goes by Stu? His mom brought him by when she saw us working. She wanted him to help. Told me to 'work him hard and don't give him a cent.' "

Me, Mom, and Maxey just stared at each other.

Mom shook her head. "Well, it's all just amazing and beautiful, Frank! I don't know what to say." She turned to him and gave him a look that I'd never seen on my mom's face before. I could see the little red hearts doing the conga around her head.

"I'm so glad you like it, Kath!" he said back, looking just as dopey. And then they hugged for a really long time. About twenty minutes.

Maxey kept flying over the maze, in and out, around and over and out, like a ballerina gone mad. "It's perfect! I love it!"

Now I tromped across the new grass and pebbles looking to see what he'd done with the one big hole. I felt all turned around because everything looked so different. I'd have to bring Nit out here tonight and have her help me. And Aurora, too, if I could pry her away from Fancy.

"Gee, it's really swell and everything. Now can I go in?" I asked.

Mom broke away from Frank. "Certainly. Why don't you go right up to your room? I'll be there in just a minute," she said, giving me the Look.

I was begging for trouble, but at this point—well, bring it on!

Chapter 31

It was 7:11, eleven very long minutes after my slumber party was supposed to start. So far no one had showed up. I chewed on a chunk of my bottom lip. Maybe Mom had called everyone and told them we were canceling because I was the most ungrateful girl who ever lived.

I got the Locker Room Talk that Mom saves for special occasions when she is very unhappy with her team's attitude. She was so disappointed in me. She made me take a time-out in my room for an hour, which meant I didn't get to write everyone's name on her cookie with the frosting shooter. I was very disappointed in *her* about that. She probably let Frank do it.

Having to save your whole family was a very big job for a fourth grader. But Mom always said that the Maloney women come from hearty stock. It was my legacy. We'd survived the Potato Famine, and a whole lot of bossing around from the entire country of England, and the Protestants, too.

I went to our bedroom window and looked out back. I could see exactly where Frank was standing out there because of all the lights. He was right next to a giant cactus with a lot of wavy arms on it near the back edge of the labyrinth. It was new from the nursery. I hadn't noticed it when I went out there earlier. I drew in my breath.

I bet that was where the giant hole used to be! He'd put a T. rex–sized cactus on top of it to mark the spot. Because if you really didn't want anyone digging up your treasure, putting a prickly cactus on top of it wasn't a bad idea at all. Frank stepped closer to it and tamped the earth around it with his foot.

Oh, yeah, *X* marks the spot!

• • •

At 7:16, the doorbell started ringing and didn't stop until everyone had arrived. Except for Aurora and Fancy, who wouldn't come until around ten o'clock.

None of the girls in my class had ever been to my house before except Nit, and all the parents stayed around until they'd made sure everything was safe. Guess they were just checking that there weren't any of my dad's pals sprung from the joint hanging around or anything.

Mom introduced Frank as her old friend from college who was helping out with the party. Everyone fell for him right away. He was so friendly that none of the grown-ups seemed like they wanted to leave. Any minute now they'd all be trooping out into the backyard for a tour. My first party would become famous in St. Dominic's history as the Worst Slumber Party Ever Where All the Parents Stayed and Prayed. I gave Mom a polite but pleading look, and she started moving them out the door.

I did a mental count to make sure everyone was there. I counted them by best-friend couples—Missy and Sissy, Kimber and Georgia, Naomi and Drew, Mary Peters and Mary Paul. And then there was Kayla Quintana, who hadn't picked a new best friend yet since she and Aurora split, and Becca, who didn't have a best friend, just her twin brother, who wasn't invited. Then me and Nit, and that was everybody!

The Marys had on twirly green skirts and matching tops. A lot of the girls were wearing green nail polish, and when the moms and dads weren't looking, Kimber lifted her shirt and showed us her green flowered beginner's bra. She hadn't really started beginning anything yet, but it was pretty and I almost wished I had one.

Nit had sprayed her hair green and then painted her eyebrows, too, which made her look even weirder than usual, but I didn't mind. And I had my green polka-dot pajamas on already, and I had taken a Magic Marker and colored my freckles green. I looked extremely dotty.

The only person who wasn't wearing green was Kayla. She looked bored already. I don't think she even wanted to come to my party, but she couldn't stand the thought of everyone being at my house without her. I had been keeping my fingers crossed all day that she wouldn't come.

It was hard for me not to just grab her by her pointy little ears and yell at her for all the trouble she'd caused at school with the singing valentine. Payback was coming!

"You guys all look very queer," Kayla said. "You're going to be very embarrassed when the boys come over."

"What boys?" I said.

She rolled her eyes at me. "From school, where do you think? Marcus always pays me to tell him when the slumber parties are. Sometimes he and his friends crash them. I guess you don't know that since this is your first party," she said, walking over to inspect the snack table.

"I don't want any boys coming over!" I said. "This is for girls only."

"Don't worry, Ef," Nit said. "She's probably bluffing."

"But what if he comes? Aurora will go ape, and it will just ruin everything."

She squeezed my hand. "Your party is going to be perfect! People will be talking about it for weeks. And I'm so glad you invited everyone!"

I gave her a big smile back. This was Nit's first slumber party too, and I could tell she was as excited as I was.

Mom and Frank came out of the kitchen loaded with the green-crust pizza. Everyone started squealing and crowded around.

"Is it going to taste green?" Mary Peters asked.

"Green doesn't have a taste, silly," Mary Paul said.

"It does too," she said. "Green tastes like lime!"

Frank laughed. "Well, you don't need to worry. It's only green colored."

Kayla shoved to the front to inspect it. "Gross. It looks like it's moldy. I'm not eating any of that," she said to Frank.

"Great," he said. "I'll take your piece, then. Feel free to go into the kitchen and make yourself a sandwich when you get hungry."

I held back a laugh. Score one for Frank.

He pulled out the pizza wheel and started slicing it up. Everyone held out their plates. Mom and Maxey brought out the all-green vegetable trays and guacamole.

Kimber took a big bite of pizza and moaned. "It's really good."

Georgia scooched up near Frank, which wasn't easy because he was getting scooched from all sides. Geez, could anyone resist the guy?

The doorbell rang again. Maxey ran to get it. I couldn't imagine who it might be. It was way too early for Aurora, and everyone was already here.

"Effie!" Maxey called. "Uh, you have another guest."

I went over to the door and Mom followed.

Donal! And he was holding a paper bag and a rolled-up blanket.

"How are ye!" he said, grinning at me and then at Mom. He stuck out his hand. "I'm Donal, and this here is my da, Jack McGuire. Very pleased to meet you!"

"Well, come in!" Mom said, trying to shake hands with "Da," who was holding his hat rolled up in one hand and a giant ham in the other.

"Kind of ya to invite my lad to your hooley," he said, handing over the ham. "It's his first invite since we moved. Couldn't git him to speak of nothing else for days."

"But—but—" I started.

Mom shushed me with a firm squeeze on my neck.

"We are so happy you could come! Donal, Effie has told me all about you. And you're just in time for our St. Patrick's Day green pizza!"

"Grand! And I brought my covers like the invite said." He

pulled a folded-up invitation out of his pocket and handed it to my mom.

"Donal," she said, taking it from him. "Why don't you go fix yourself a plate while I get acquainted with your dad?"

He headed inside, then turned quick. "Da, just look!" he said, grinning and pointing to the decorations. "There's St. Patty and shamrocks everywhere. Just like the oul' pub back home!"

"Jack," Mom said. "Can I get you something to drink?"

"No, thank you, ma'am, I best be off!"

"Wait," she said. "I'm afraid there's been a bit of a misunderstanding. I didn't want to embarrass Donal, but this is a girls' sleepover. There aren't any boys coming. I'm not sure how this happened—he can stay for dinner, of course, but then—I suppose I could bring him home later?"

Donal's dad turned bright red and rolled his cap into a twist. "Aaach, I feel like an arse. The boy told me he'd been invited for a sleeper. Showed me the invite."

I pulled it from Mom's hand and looked at it. It was just a copy. Didn't have a pink bow on it or anything. "This wasn't meant for him. I don't know how he got it. I'm so sorry."

"Well, I'm working the night shift, and I didn't do the arranging for Mrs. Mulbury to come for him. I don't know if I can still reach her."

Kayla strutted over then, nibbling on a stick of celery. She looked at my mom. "It's so nice of you to let him stay, Coach Maloney," she said. "This is his first party, you know. Sister Emmanuel has asked all of us to do *whatever* we can to make Donal feel welcome in our country."

I smelled a rat. A big blond one. She'd invited him. Just to try to ruin my party!

"Well, actually, Kayla, I'm just not sure—" Mom started.

"Oh, please, PRETTY PLEASE, Coach!" she said, her voice growing louder. "You HAVE to let him stay!" She turned and gave her girls the nod for backup.

Missy, Sissy, Becca, and Drew hurried right over. "Ooh, yes! We want him to stay. Please! Please!"

Mom looked at me, then back at Donal, who was standing under the banner having his picture taken with the Marys. Looking like he'd just won the lottery.

"You know what, Jack?" Mom said. "We're going to make this work. We'll just have him sleep upstairs. Don't you give it another thought. We'd be delighted to have him as our guest!"

"If you're sure now," he said.

"Yes!" I choked. "Our pleasure."

"I'll be back in the morning then to collect my boyo. If he starts actin' up, give him a bit of a swat. He'll come around. Right, then, I'm off!" he said, backing off the porch.

"Good girl," Mom said through clenched teeth as we kept our smiles plastered on and waved him good-bye. She gave me a squeeze around the shoulders. "Thanks again for the ham, Jack!" she called.

She looked down at me. "We're going to laugh about this someday."

Chapter 32

Donal grabbed a piece of pizza and sank his teeth into it. He moaned with happiness, looking around. "Where's the lads, then? Outside?"

"There's no boys here, Donal," Kimber said.

"Just me?" he asked, incredulous.

"That's right," Kayla said. "You're our very special guest!"

"I'm right gobsmacked," he said, slapping his forehead. "Must be the luck of the Irish."

Frank came over and put his arm around him. "I'm Frank, and I must say I'm very happy to have another man here with me tonight. I was feeling quite outnumbered."

"So, do you live here, Frank?" Kayla asked.

"No, I'm just a temporary houseguest."

"Are you Coach's boyfriend?" Kimber asked.

"We're just old friends," he said, rolling the pizza cutter through another pie.

"Are you a coach, too?" from Sissy.

"Nope," he said, putting the last piece out on a plate.

"What do you do, then?" Georgia asked.

"Well, lately, I've been doing a bit of gardening."

I shot a glance at Maxey, who as usual was hanging on his every word, even though she was supposed to help serve and then get lost.

"Okay, ladies and gent," Frank said, trying to back out of the clutch. "My work is done here. I'm going to retire to the kitchen. I have a Scrabble date with Effie's mom and Maxey, and you kids have a very fun party to get to. Donal, if you start feeling outranked, come out to the kitchen and join me."

"Good-o, Frank!" he said.

"Oh! Don't leave," Missy said.

"You can stay!" the Marys pleaded.

I pulled Nit close to me. "Get them all in the living room. I need to talk to my mother! I can't believe Donal came."

"In here, everyone!" Nit said, motioning them to follow.

I burst through the swinging door into the kitchen. Mom was setting up the Scrabble board.

"Mom!" I whispered in a strangled voice. "What are we going to do about Donal? We can't sleep with a *boy* here! What if the parents or Sister Emmanuel hear about this?"

"Leave all that to me. They'll understand. Donal can sleep up in your room. Maxey will sleep with me. It will all be perfectly proper."

"This is terrible!"

"Only if you let it be, Ef. That's up to you. Now get out there with your guests."

· · ·

Mom had moved all the furniture back so we'd have a place to dance, hang out, and lay our sleeping bags. Everyone plopped down on the floor with their pizza and snacks.

Maxey followed us in with a big pitcher of green punch and set it on the table. "Did you all say grace yet?" she asked.

Kids stopped with their pizza midway to their mouths.

"Maxey!" I said in my sternest voice. "Go away!" I leaned over and turned up the music. "Just ignore her, everyone."

Mom must have heard me because she came right out and pulled Maxey away.

"I really could use some help in the kitchen, Maxey."

"When did your sister turn into such a wacko?" Kayla asked, reaching over to pull a slice of pepperoni off Naomi's pizza. She popped it into her mouth and sucked her finger clean.

"She was just pulling your leg, Kayla!" Nit said. "I can't believe you fell for that."

Kayla's cheeks got red. "Oh, really? I'm not so sure about that! She's acting so holy at school that there's a rumor the nuns might pick her to be May Queen. And you know being May Queen, or even an FMQ—Future May Queen—is the kiss of death at St. Dom's. Might as well join the convent. No boy would ever like her after that." She reached over to Naomi's plate again, but Naomi held it over her head.

"Get your own, you mooch!" she said.

"Oh, fine," she said. "Anyway, I heard that Phil didn't even want to come over tonight for a sleepover with Maxey. Guess she told Maxey that she was home sick, but Marcy says she is really going to the movies with some girls from their class."

I looked over at Nit, who wouldn't meet my eyes. Oh, man, it must be true.

"We gonna play spin the bottle, then?" Donal asked, wiping some pizza sauce off his face with his sleeve. "I read aboat it in a book."

"*Noooo!*" the Marys shrieked. "The nuns told us we're not ever to play that."

"So, Effie, what are we going to do tonight?" Kimber asked. "Are we going to play games? Did you rent movies for us? When we were at Mary Peters's party, after we got back from our limousine ride to Buffalo Bill's Steakhouse, we watched movies all night long! And," she said, looking around to make sure none of the adults were lurking, "her big brother gave us a movie that was rated R to watch after the parents went to sleep!"

"But it was such a dumb movie," Georgia said.

"We're going to have *so* much fun!" I said with a big smile, trying to get the image of their limo ride out of my mind. "My mom borrowed a DVD player and rented two movies for us."

"You guys don't have a DVD player?" Becca asked.

"No," I said. "But we're getting one real soon."

"Me and my da don't have one either," Donal pitched in. "We've just a telly."

"What movies did she get?" Mary Paul asked.

"Well, since this is an Irish party, we got this hilarious old movie called *Darby O'Gill and the Little People*, and then a brand-new movie about St. Therese the Little Flower. We can count that one for Angel Scout Religious Study credit. Mom checked with Sister Lucille."

The room went dead quiet until Nit broke in. "Wow, that's so cool! I saw *Darby O'Gill* once—it's hilarious," she said.

"Was it even made in this century?" Kayla mocked. She looked smug as a bug at the expressions on the girls' faces. "So, Effie, what are the party favors? Pencils and walnuts?"

Missy clicked her tongue. "Kayla, you're not supposed to ask. That's so rude!"

"Pardon moi!" she said, at her snottiest.

My lips felt dry and I took a big drink of punch. "We're doing tons more stuff, too. We're going to make friendship bracelets. Donal, you could make a key chain, I suppose, or a necklace. We have lots of beads in all colors, and that really good jewelry twine that won't break. We even bought alphabet beads so you can spell out your friend's name if you want."

"Oh, fun," Mary Peters said in a voice that made it sound like it wasn't fun at all.

"Didn't we make friendship bracelets at Kimber's second-grade party?" Kayla asked. She didn't wait for an answer but went over and flopped down on the couch with her feet up on it. She grabbed a magazine off the table. "Call me if anything interesting happens," she said, pretending to yawn.

"Ignore her," Georgia said. "She's like this at all the parties, unless it's her own."

"Shut up, Georgia," Kayla said from behind her magazine. "Well, it's not my fault," she said. "You all play such baby games. I've outgrown that stuff."

"Making friendship bracelets and watching movies is just

what we're doing *first*," I jumped in. "What we're doing after that is definitely not for babies," I said.

All eyes were on me now. Kayla looked over at me with a smirk. "Are we going to sneak out with your sister and go to Mass?"

"We're walking the labyrinth."

She dropped her magazine on her lap. "What is that?"

Nit jumped in. "Just about the scariest and spookiest thing you've ever done in your life, is all!"

"That's right," I said. "But we can't do it until midnight."

Chapter 33

After we had all eaten enough pizza and green food to last us a lifetime, and watched the St. Therese movie, Nit and I passed out all the party-favor bags. Nit gave up hers so Donal could have one. While everyone went through them, I set up the beads to make our bracelets. Nit pulled me aside and whispered that maybe the reason Kayla didn't want to make a friendship bracelet was because she didn't have anyone to give it to.

"You're right," I whispered back. That's why I love Nit. She's the most thoughtful girl. But was it any wonder Kayla didn't have any friends? She made trouble wherever she went!

Everybody was busy sorting out their loot, putting on their tattoos, and popping chocolates into their mouths.

"Thanks for the bags, Effie!" Kimber said.

"Hey! I've got a holy card in mine," Mary Peters said with a frown in her voice.

My stomach did a nosedive. "Then you win!" I said, in a rush.

She raised her arms over her head, victorious. "Yippeee! What did I win?"

I looked at Nit. She looked back at me. "You get first dibs on the bathroom in the morning."

"Ohhh, lucky!" Mary Paul said.

The doorbell rang just then and I jumped up. "That must be Aurora!"

I ran to the door and flung it open.

It was a priest!

"Well, hello, young lady! I'm Monsignor Finnegan." He held out his hand. "I'd like to speak with Father Avila."

Oh, no, not now. As much as I wanted to get rid of Frank, I did not want the girls to find out that we had been hiding a disobedient priest in our house!

I slipped out onto the porch and pulled the door closed behind me and held it. "Do you think you could come back tomorrow?" I said. "I'm having a slumber party right now. We're all so busy!"

"Oh, what fun! Is it your birthday, young lady?"

I shook my head. "No, it's for St. Patrick. But it's my first party, and I really don't want anything to go wrong."

"Oh, it won't, I'm sure of it! Why don't you just go ask Father if he could join me outside, and no one will be the wiser."

"You're not going to put him in handcuffs, are you?" I whispered, my stomach filling up with dread. "I mean, since he ran away without permission and all."

He leaned over, looked around, then whispered back, "No, I'll probably just give him a hug. Is that all right with you?"

The door pulled inward behind me and I almost fell in. Some of the girls crowded around.

"It's not Aurora!" Kimber said.

"Hello, Father," the Marys said in unison.

Mom came up behind all of us. She put a hand on my shoulder. I could feel her stiffen when she saw who it was.

"Ah, you must be Katherine—hello! At last! I'm Monsignor Finnegan. May I call you Kath? I've heard so much about you over the years from Frank."

She reached out a hand. "Monsignor, a pleasure. Um, come in, please," she said, not sounding entirely convinced.

Mom turned toward us. "Girls, go on back to your party. We're going to go into the kitchen. We won't be in your way one bit."

"Splendid," Monsignor said, stepping inside. "Is Father Avila in there?" he asked.

"Not unless he came down the chimney," Kayla said. "They've just got their gardener, Frank, in there."

"Oh, I see," he said, looking over at Mom.

"Nit," I said, "get them started on the beads, will you? I'll be right there."

Nit's eyes looked a little dazed. "Yeah, okay." And then, softly to me, "Is Frank a priest?"

"Yeah," I said as I headed off into the kitchen.

Frank and Maxey were laughing over the Scrabble board when we all trooped in. Frank looked up, and his expression froze.

"Frank," Monsignor said. "I'm so glad to see you!"

Frank crossed the room toward him. Monsignor pulled him into a bear hug.

"I've missed you. All of us have missed you, Frank," he repeated, clapping him on the back. Over and over.

Frank still seemed stunned. Finally, he said, "Monsignor! I certainly wasn't expecting you here. You've surprised me. I didn't—well, I—I'm very surprised. How did you know to come here?"

"Someone called. They thought you might need me."

"But who?" Frank said.

"It doesn't matter," he said. "I'm just glad to see you—to see that you're all right."

"Girls, let's give them some privacy so they can talk," Mom said. "We'll be upstairs if you need us. Effie, you need to get back to your party."

I didn't move. On account of someone had nailed my feet to the ground.

Frank looked at me. "It's fine, Effie. Go have fun." His eyes lingered on me a moment, gentle.

So I couldn't figure out why, then, his look burned a hole right to my heart.

· · ·

When the doorbell rang about thirty minutes later, followed by the sound of a basketball dribbling on the porch, I felt crazy with relief. I hadn't been able to concentrate on the party since the monsignor had arrived. But Nit was doing a bang-up job of keeping things going. She was telling really frightful vampire stories. Everyone was eating them up.

I raced to the door and threw it open. "Aurora, I'm so glad you're here!"

"Hi, Effie!" she said with her big smile.

I looked behind her. "Where's Fancy? Didn't she come with you?" I asked, my heart ready to take off in big happy swoons.

"She's on the lawn."

I looked around her. "Well, what's she doing out there?"

Aurora giggled. "She's sitting on top of Booger Boy. He was in the bushes when we came up to the front door. She dragged him off and is having a little talk with him."

"Really?"

"Yes," Aurora said, looking quite pleased. "She's so great."

My heart took a small dive. "Well, if I would have known he was out here, I would have beaten him to a pulp," I said with a huff.

The rest of the girls came flocking to the door then, and peered out.

"Hi, Aurora!" they yelled.

"Hey, Triboni! Come here!" came a voice from the lawn.

"What's going on out there?" Kimber asked, shading her eyes from the porch light. "Who is that giant girl and what is she sitting on?"

I nearly got plowed off the porch as the girls streamed out of the house.

Nit and I took up the back.

"Evenin', ladies," Booger Boy said, trying to act all casual.

"Boger Boy!" Donal said. "What the divil are you doing?"

"Just dropped by, when I got mauled by this *ox* sitting on top of me." He tried to move her hand from his throat, but she had a death clamp on it.

"Everyone," I said, remembering my manners, "this is Aurora's team captain, Fancy. Fancy, this is everyone—Mary

Peters, Mary Paul, Kimber, Georgia, Naomi, Drew, Missy, Becca, Sissy, and Kayla is still inside—"

"Pretending she isn't interested," Nit added.

"Right, and you've already met Nit and me, of course."

"H'lo, everyone," Fancy said. Then she looked at Aurora. "This the kid that you got expelled over? What do you want me to do with him?"

"She didn't get expelled!" I said.

Aurora shrugged. "I dunno. What do you guys think? He's probably been out here in the hedges all night spying on the party. What's a good punishment for that?"

"You could make him watch that St. Therese flick," Donal suggested. "It's bloody deadly!"

"I haven't been here all night," he said. "Just long enough to catch that priest cat show up—*girl*-let-me-breathe-will-you?"

Fancy backed it off a smidge. Then she leaned over him and put her mouth real close. "Here's some breath for you. I had two full orders of onion rings tonight. Plus the rest of Aurora's."

"Knock it off!" he yelled. "You're killing me! C'mon, let's make a deal."

"I don't exactly think you're in any kind of bargaining position, boy," she said.

"Whatever, get off me!"

"Why?" she said. "I'm having fun here!"

I actually felt kind of bad for him, now that I knew he hadn't been the one making fun of Aurora or falling in love with her and stuff. But he had been spying on my party! For that, he needed to pay. And I had an idea about how he could.

But I just needed to get Fancy off him so he wouldn't get too mad and refuse to help me.

"Fancy, there's cake inside," I said.

She jumped up and hurried toward the house.

• • •

After being saved from a likely fatal thrashing by Fancy, Booger Boy didn't need much coaxing to agree to play a part in the planning for the Midnight Labyrinth Walk. We needed him to pull it off. He'd gone home for a while but was planning on sneaking back later to help us out. I also whispered to him not to say anything about Kayla framing him in front of Aurora. I promised him we would figure out a way to get her back for it. Just not tonight.

Frank and Monsignor Finnegan had gone out for a walk so they could talk. They were gone for the longest time, but I was glad. Having a monsignor in the house would have put kind of a crimp in the party. Little did the girls know we had two priests in the house!

We put on the *Darby O'Gill* movie to pass the time until midnight. As luck, finally, would have it, Donal knew the entire movie by heart and had everyone in hysterics doing the Irish jig and performing all the songs.

Fancy parked her chair by the snack table and Hoovered up every remaining morsel. She was a very hungry girl. Didn't say too much, though. I imagine going to a party with fourth graders was probably boring her to tears. Aurora said not to worry about it because she really enjoyed sitting on Booger Boy, and she loved the green cake. And she'd swept up all the unused tattoos and had herself plastered with them like a circus lady.

She was pretty starstruck over my mom, too. The St. Ignatius team Mom coached went to the finals nearly every year. Fancy said it was her dream to play on my mom's team someday, even though they were Catholics and she wasn't. She started to spin her basketball on her finger to show off, but Mom grabbed it from her and told her to put it in the garage.

"No basketballs in the house tonight!" she said.

"Yes, ma'am!" Fancy said.

Chapter 34

By eleven-thirty p.m., all of us were sacked out in our sleeping bags on the living-room floor. Eyes closed. Missy and Sissy were snoring.

All accounted for.

Well, except for Donal, whom Mom had taken upstairs under protest. When he'd come waltzing out of the downstairs bathroom wearing only what he called his "Y-fronts," Mom had put him in a big old bathrobe and taken him away.

The girls shrieked and then fell into complete hysterical laughter at him standing there in his tightie whities. It wasn't his fault that he didn't know boys weren't supposed to be seen like that in front of their girl classmates. Maybe his "da" never told him. And I wasn't sure yet if there was a "ma" to go with the "da."

By the time Mom got Donal settled and came back down one more time to check on us, we were all deep in Slumber Land like little angels.

Some of us faking, of course.

Maxey and Kayla snuck right off to the downstairs bathroom and locked the door. Maxey told me that she had promised Kayla she'd give her an updo and she didn't want anyone watching. Fine, whatever.

And even though I was "absolutely knackered," as Donal would say, I still had my reputation as a party host to finish the night on a high note. And I had the tiny flame of hope in my heart that maybe Aurora would have so much fun with us, she'd tell her mom she just had to come back to St. Dom's. I stuck one of the paper shamrocks under my pillow and one under Nit's, too. Couldn't hurt!

I nudged Nit next to me.

Her eyes flew open. She wiped at a dribble of drool coming from her mouth. "Sorry! Is it time?"

"Not quite yet," I whispered. "But come outside."

We tiptoed over the bodies spread out all over the floor. A couple of girls whispered to us, "Do we get up now? Is it time?"

"Shhh! Not yet. We'll be back for you."

We snuck out as quietly as we could. I'd asked Mom to leave the labyrinth lights on all night so it wouldn't be so dark in the living room, in case anyone was scared but didn't want to admit it.

I led Nit over the stepping-stones to the rear, where the

T. rex cactus was. "I think Frank might have buried something right under here. Can you tell? You're such a pro at finding things, Nit. I know this isn't exactly something 'lost,' since we don't know what it is. But can you tell if there's something here that doesn't belong? Maybe here, or around here?"

Nit squatted down near the base and was quiet for a long minute. Then she got up. "Let me walk around a bit."

She walked all through the yard, and then moved to the labyrinth. I watched her move across the stones slowly, one by one, following the circular paths of it. She stayed in the middle for a bit, then came back out, one stone at a time. I hugged myself against the chill.

"Something's here," she said, when she joined me again. She shivered and then rubbed her arms with her hands to try to warm herself. "But I don't think it's a treasure. It feels more like—I don't know—more like a . . ."

"What? Like a what?"

She turned and looked at me. "It's more like a . . . well, sort of like a death."

"A death? OMIGOD! Did he bury somebody out here?"

"No!" she said. "Not a murder kind of death. More like a very sad kind of death."

"A dead gopher?"

"No." She walked back over to the cactus. Ran her fingers over a nonprickly place.

"Is there something under here or not?"

"I think there might be, Ef, but leave it alone."

"Are you kidding? 'Leave it alone'?"

"I don't think it's what you're looking for. It's very sad and private."

"I'm getting a shovel."

"No!" she said. "I mean it, Effie. You've got to leave this alone. Trust me."

"I'm digging it up tomorrow."

"Well, count me out, Effie," Nit said. "You're on your own with this."

I looked at her, shocked. "You said you'd help me—remember? Back at the hospital?"

"I did help you, just like I said I would. And I gave you my opinion. Frank seems like a really nice guy, and now that I know he's a priest, that clears up the thing I thought he was hiding. There is something out here, but it's not a treasure. You should leave it alone. *Don't*—dig—it—up."

"I can't leave it alone. Now he's got you under his spell! He's got something out here, and I need to get to it before he ruins my mom's life!"

Nit got in my face then. "You know what I really hate?" she said. "I hate it when people ask me about something, and if what I say doesn't agree with what they want to hear, they decide I must be wrong."

"You think you know everything, Nit! You don't! You're dead wrong about him, and if you were really my best friend, you'd help me! I'll get Aurora to help me. *She* won't let me down."

Nit stared at me like I'd hauled off and smacked her. Then she just shook her head. "I'm going to sleep. When I wake up, I'm going home. I'm not speaking to you again until you're ready to apologize for that. That was beneath you."

I crossed my arms over my chest. Didn't say a word.

• • •

My head was throbbing when I woke up. I looked at the clock on the living-room wall. It wasn't quite seven a.m. Everyone was still sleeping. I looked over at Nit's sleeping bag and she was gone. But there was a note sticking out of it. I grabbed it.

Effeline, please thank your mother for her hospitality. I'm walking home. Tell her not to worry. I'll call her to let her know I got home safe.

But she didn't even sign it or put any *X*s or *O*s on it like she usually did. She was really mad at me. I rolled over on my back and the last few hours flashed through my mind.

The Midnight Labyrinth Walk was wildly successful. Everyone loved it. Even Kayla cracked a couple of guffaws over it. She didn't want to do the walk herself, so she helped me. She had a big plastic bag wrapped over her hair, which looked really dumb, but she said it was to protect her new hairstyle while she slept.

Kayla and I each took a person outside one by one and put a blindfold on her. We told her that she had to walk the entire labyrinth without skipping a single stone, and she had to make it all the way to the center and back. Even if something scary happened while she was out there.

Which was exactly what we had planned for them. Booger Boy was out there in the yard, lurking in a dark cape he'd brought and making chilling, sinister noises.

Of course it woke up Mom right away, but I talked her into letting us finish so everyone got a turn. Fortunately, Mom didn't see that it was Booger Boy out there, or she would have called his mother straight away to pick him up. Donal slept through the whole thing. Mom told me Frank had gone out for a drive with the monsignor after their walk and hadn't come back yet.

Fancy was the last to go, but when she got near the middle and Booger Boy started huffing and snorting, she grabbed him and threw him down in some kind of martial arts move. Even with her blindfold on.

He wanted to go home after that. You could hardly blame him. He'd had a long night.

So had I. I couldn't wait until breakfast was over and everyone went home. Frank had promised to make all of us Macadamia French Toast with green bread—I stopped and caught my breath. Frank! I wondered what time he had come back. I hadn't heard him come in, but I'd been dead to the world.

I slid out of my sleeping bag and tiptoed over to Mom's office. Cracked the door open soft as I could.

The couch was all made up nice and tidy. All his personal stuff was still on the shelf.

I padded out to the kitchen. Maybe he was in there getting breakfast ready for us and being superquiet.

The kitchen was cold and empty.

I ran to the front window and looked out. Frank's car was gone. And I didn't see an extra car out there that looked like it belonged to a monsignor. If the two of them had gone out for a drive last night, they wouldn't have taken both cars.

My heart thumped under my ribs.

Father Frank had flown the coop! I should have been happy.

Chapter 35

All thirteen of us and Mom skidded to a stop at the bathroom door to find Kayla Quintana standing in front of the mirror, clutching her hair in gobs and shrieking. Pieces of foil were strewn all over the countertop and a stinky black plastic bag lay in the sink.

"LOOK WHAT SHE DID TO MY *HAIR!*" she yelled at Mom.

Mom pushed through the mob of girls and stared.

Kayla had gotten more than an updo. She had black streaks running all through her hair and a giant set of inky bangs.

"Did *Maxey* do this to you?" she asked.

"YES!"

"While you were sleeping?" Mom asked, spinning Kayla from front to back, like maybe there was a better side to it.

"No! Not when I was *sleeping*. She did it before the Labyrinth Walk. She told me my hair was really pretty, but it would look better with highlights. She said she could give them to me for free. But I wanted blond highlights, not BLACK ones! My mother is going to kill me! And then she is going to kill all of you! We're going to sue!"

My mom put the toilet seat down. "Sit!" she barked at Kayla.

And then, "MAXINE MALONEY, GET DOWN HERE RIGHT NOW!"

• • •

I was outside sweeping and raking the labyrinth when Frank called later that day. Mom had had a fit when she saw what a mess we'd made of it the night before, playing Haunted Labyrinth. After having to spend $85.00 plus tip to get Kayla's hair back to normal and trying to calm Mrs. Quintana down, she was kind of cranky. Mom told Maxey that she would not be getting any more birthday presents or her own slumber party until she turned thirty.

It was actually the second time Frank had called. He had left a text message on Mom's cell late last night, saying he wouldn't be back until the next day, and would she mind making the slumber-party breakfast. When he called again around lunchtime, Maxey came running outside to tell me. Not because she wanted to keep me in the loop, but because she couldn't hold her excitement. "It's him!" she said. "Mom's on the phone with Frank right now!"

I shrugged like it didn't matter to me one way or the other. But my heart began to race, and it wasn't from the raking.

I kept staring at the cactus and its long, wavy arms. Tried

to figure out how I could dig it up without becoming its personal pincushion. The thing was as big as me. It really was a two-person job. Nit wouldn't help me, obviously. Aurora was busy with basketball and homework all the rest of the weekend. And I had a feeling that where Aurora went these days, Fancy wouldn't be far behind. I really didn't feel like bringing an outsider in on this.

Which left me with just one option. Maxey.

I just had to figure out how I could get her to help me. I had a slightly better chance these days since she wasn't really in her right mind. I was starting to work out a plan when Mom called us in for a huddle.

We sat in our regular Team Meeting places on the couch. Her nose was a little red, like maybe she had been crying or was trying not to. She really was having the worst day ever. I balled my fists at my sides.

"Well, that was Frank," she said. "First of all, he wanted to make sure he apologized to you both for leaving the party and leaving all the work to us. He feels very bad about that."

"Well, he just left for the night, right? That's okay," Maxey said. "What time will he be home?"

"He's coming by in just a bit to get his things."

We both stared at her like she'd just said that in Swahili and we couldn't understand a word she was saying.

"What things?" Maxey asked.

"His suitcase," Mom said. "And I wanted to give you both a little time to prepare for that. I know this might be a little hard."

"Hard!" Maxey said, starting to sound hysterical. "Oh, no, not hard at all! Effie, is this hard for you?"

My brain wouldn't cooperate.

"I know, Max," Mom said. "I feel sad about it too."

"We need to pray right *now* that we can convince him to stay when he gets here," Maxey said. She reached for our hands and grabbed them tight.

I yanked mine away. "I don't want him back!"

"It's all your fault," she yelled at me. "If you weren't such a brat, he would stay. You didn't even try!"

"Maxey, cool it!" Mom barked. "I know you're upset. But you're being completely unfair. We can pray for him, if you like, but not to come back. Just that he'll be happy wherever he is."

"But he's going back with his monsignor to church, right?" I asked.

"I don't know," she said, pinching the bridge of her nose. She looked so sad and tired. "I really and absolutely don't know."

• • •

I did not want to talk to Frank when he came back. I put a big sign on my door that said "I'm sleeping! Do not disturb! No matter what!" I heard him come up the stairs and stand outside my door a minute. He called my name real soft, but I ignored him.

About a half hour later, I heard a rustle of paper under my door, and then I heard our VW pull out. Which made no sense. Was Mom leaving us too?

I raced to the window and looked out, and saw Frank driving our old car away.

I went and grabbed the note that had come under the door.

Dear Effie,

I'm sorry that we didn't get to talk today. And I'm really sorry that I missed the rest of your party. Your mom told me all about the scary Midnight Labyrinth Walk. Sounded so fun! See? You've already found your own way to make it useful to you. That makes me really happy.

Monsignor Finnegan has requested that I take a couple of weeks on retreat, away from here, to sort things out. That's probably a good idea. I owe him at least that.

I'll be back soon to see the three of you, Effie. You have my word on that.

> *Love,*
> *Frank*

• • •

Mom tried to cheer us up later by telling us she was going to pick up our favorite take-out hamburgers, jumbo shakes, and curly fries, even though it wasn't even Take-out Sunday. And wouldn't it be fun to drive in Frank's nice car that he left us? He took our Bug because he wanted to work on the engine while he was gone. I guess retreat didn't mean you only prayed all day long. I was very mad that he took our car, because I'd left my library book in the backseat.

Maxey was too busy praying in our room to go with her, and I told her I was just too tired. Guess Mom figured we were way too beat to get into any more trouble while she was gone, so she let us stay home alone. She told Maxey not to even think about touching my hair.

I also talked her into going by the library to talk to Miss Gilbert about *Theodosia and the Serpents of Chaos* book she was never going to get back. And just to be on the safe side, I asked Mom if she'd go by the grocery store and get Pretty Girl some treats, because she looked very depressed about Frank leaving.

And those were all the excuses I could think of to keep Mom out of the house as long as possible. I wasn't sure how much time I'd need to chop that cactus down.

I barreled up the stairs to our bedroom the minute Mom pulled out of the driveway. But then I tried to catch my breath and act all cool so Maxey wouldn't know that I desperately needed her to help me. Usually, if she knows you wanted something really bad, there's no way you're going to get it. Not without paying big bucks.

She was sitting on her bed reading.

"Maxey, did you give Kayla black highlights on purpose, or was it a mistake?"

"I wouldn't make a big mistake like that! When it comes to hair, I know exactly what I'm doing!"

"Why'd you do it, then?" I asked. "You must have known you'd get in trouble."

"She kept trying to ruin your party. The girl had it coming."

I didn't know what to say. I wasn't used to Maxey looking out for me like that. "Wull, gee, Maxey . . ."

"God, I hope you're not going to try to hug me or anything," she said. "It was no big deal. Plus, I really wanted to see what would happen if you left foil on all night with a dark dye."

I looked at the bunny clock on our wall. I was losing minutes here gabbing. "If I let you do my hair this afternoon, could you help me with something?"

"Mom would kill me," she said.

"Not highlights—just comb it and stuff. I'll even let you trim my bangs."

"Really?"

"Yees, but you have to help me right now."

"Okay," she said, banging her book closed. "What's the favor?"

I had this whole whopper of a story planned about why I needed to dig up the big cactus. But I just couldn't. I didn't have the heart for it.

"I need you to help me dig up a cactus out back. Frank buried something under it, and I need to find out what it is. And before Mom gets home."

Maxey sprang from the bed, pulling me behind her. My feet never even touched the ground.

Chapter 36

We grabbed some tools from the garage—big gardening gloves, a couple of shovels, and a saw. I was hoping not to have to amputate the thing, but I would if I had to.

"The ground is still pretty soft, so it shouldn't be too hard. And the roots haven't had much time to spread out," I said.

"What do you think he buried?" Maxey asked, her voice tense and excited. "Did you see him bury it?"

"I saw him here after he buried it," I said. "I'm sure of it."

"Maybe it's his will and he's left us all something after he dies. Or a secret map to where he's gone on retreat. I tried to get him to tell me where he was going, but he wouldn't."

We both put on our gloves like doctors getting ready for surgery. "Let's see if we can just push it over," I said.

We squatted on opposite sides of it, grabbed it near the base, and tried to move it back and forth like a loose tooth. It didn't budge.

"I think it's buried too deep for that," Maxey said. "Let's try the shovels."

We dug deep all around the base and then tried rocking it back and forth again. This time we got a little sway going. "More digging!" I said, getting short of breath.

We dug.

We pushed.

Puulled.

Dug like frantic prairie dogs.

Then rocked it back and forth, forth and back.

"OUCH!" we both yelled when we slammed ourselves against one of its wavy arms and it stung us like an army of mad bees.

Maxey got down on her knees in the hole and took a small hand shovel to the base. I grabbed the saw in frustration. Enough was enough. I was going to saw the sucker down. I took a first swipe at it, and it leaked from the gash.

"Effie!" Maxey said. "I think I've got something!"

I threw down the saw and crouched next to her. She was clawing around something long and narrow. She yanked it from the dirt. "Look!" she said.

It was about the size of a big book, all wrapped up in brown paper and tied up with string.

"Give it to me!" I said, and grabbed it from her. It was way smaller than I thought it would be. What kind of treasure could be this small, I wondered? It was wrapped in layer after layer of paper, and when I got it all unwrapped, it was a black leather case with a zipper all around it.

A zipper. Not a keyhole that needed a beautiful ruby key to unlock it.

"Open it, Ef," Maxey breathed into my ear.

I pulled the zipper around slowly. I swallowed, then lifted the top back.

Neither of us spoke. We stared.

It was Frank's priest collar. And, under that, his wedding ring to God.

Chapter 37

Maxey grabbed the case from me and searched the bottom. "Is that it? Is there anything else? Why isn't there a note or anything?"

"Because he wasn't expecting anyone to dig this up!" I said through clenched teeth.

"But what does this mean?"

I glared at her. "Get a clue, Nancy Drew! What do you think? He just broke up with God!"

"He did *not*! Let's just put it back," she said, refolding the collar and zipping the box. She picked up the paper and rewrapped it as best she could. "He doesn't mean it, anyway. Maybe these are spares—an extra set—and he wanted to keep them here for safekeeping."

"Maxey," I started.

"Oh, just be quiet," she said, shoving the package back in the dirt. "Here, help me bury this. He can't know we know!"

I climbed out of the hole. "You can stick it back, but it doesn't make it go away. He's not going back to the church."

"He *has* to!" Maxey yelled.

"Why do you even care?" I shouted right back. "I thought you wanted to marry him someday—or have Mom marry him! Or have him stay with us!"

"I do! I don't!" she sputtered. "I don't know! I just don't want him to break his vows! Men should keep their promises!"

"Well, they *don't*!"

I backed away and tripped over the shovel. I landed hard on a big stone and bonked my head. I said a terrible bad cussword.

"Effie!" Maxey said, shocked.

I got to my feet and grabbed the shovel. I flung it from me as far as I could.

It landed right splat in the middle of the labyrinth. It lay there, pointing like the needle of a compass. Pointing right at me.

The back door of the house opened, and Mom stuck out her head. "I'm home, girls!" She looked out at us and the mess we'd made. "What's going on out here?"

Maxey came hurtling out of the hole and ran straight past Mom and into the house. She didn't say a word. I could hear her tearing up the staircase like she used to, and then our bedroom door slammed—hard. The house shook at the hit.

"Effie, what happened?" Mom asked, hurrying toward me. "Did you girls have a fight?"

I stared back at the shovel, its nose still fixed on me. I felt dazed from its pull, like it was really magnetic. All the questions and suspicions I had about who had hidden or stolen what swirled around in my head. I felt dizzy and crazy inside.

When Mom came up next to me, I shouted at her like we were right in the middle of an argument. "Did Dad bury some of the stolen loot out here? *Did* he?"

"*Whaaat?*"

"You know! The money he and Mr. Hocker embezzled. Did he or didn't he bury some of it out here? I need to know!"

"Effie, where did you ever get such an idea? Oh, my God," she said, looking around at all the tools we'd pulled out of the garage. "Are you girls out here digging for that?"

I lifted my shoulder and winced with pain. I'd banged it hard when I fell over the shovel.

"Just tell me! Could he have?" I asked.

"No! Effie, your father would not have buried any money out here. First off, all the embezzled money was moved electronically, and the prosecutor was able to track every dime of it. None of the money ever came into our home, or the Hockers' home. Which was the only blessing in that ugly mess."

The truth of what she said cut through the mental fog. "Oh," I said, dragging in a deep breath. "I just thought maybe . . ."

Mom shook her head. "No—there's nothing out here! What in the world would make the two of you start digging now, especially after Frank did all this beautiful work?"

She looked at the big saw mark on the cactus. "Oh, no! Look what you girls have done! This cactus probably cost him a couple hundred dollars. I hope you didn't hurt it."

"It's fine," I said, jumping back into the hole. "We'll fix it. You can just go back inside."

She looked at me, suspicious. "All right, young lady, spill it. *Now*."

I lowered my eyes. "I thought Frank was looking for something out here—you know, maybe he thought Dad had buried money." I hesitated, then stopped.

"Go on!"

"I figured that the labyrinth was just an excuse so he could dig up our yard. It made the perfect cover."

"You've got to be kidding, Ef. How could you ever think Frank would do such a thing?" She kept shaking her head like it just wouldn't compute. "This does not make sense. He dug up the whole yard already. So why are you and Maxey out here digging up this poor cactus?"

I tried to think of a good answer to that. And I could still feel the sharp nose of the shovel pointed straight at me.

"I thought Frank was either trying to find a treasure, or that maybe . . ." I dug the toe of my sneaker around in the dirt, trying to find what I needed to say.

"Maybe what?" Mom lifted up my chin with a firm finger so I'd look at her.

"I thought Frank might be out here burying something."

"What in the world would he possibly be burying out in our yard?"

"Loot," I mumbled.

"Loot?"

I nodded, then tucked my chin in.

"What kind of loot, Effie?" she asked, shocked.

"Church loot, like maybe some money he stole from the collections, or fancy church art." My eyes started to burn. I pulled on the cord around my neck and lifted the key from under my shirt. "Something that fit in a treasure box. I took this key from his room a while back."

Mom held it between her fingers, then looked at me. Blew out a gust of breath she'd been holding.

I went on. "But I wanted to find the loot first and make Frank give it back before you found out. I didn't want another man you loved to have to go to jail." One hot tear went overboard and landed in the dirt. Left a dark wet spot.

"Oh, Effie" was all she said, and she stepped into the hole and pulled me next to her.

I lay my forehead in the hard, reassuring center of her.

"Not all men are bad guys," she whispered. After a long quiet moment, she said, "But I guess I understand why you might think they are."

My nose began to run, and she wiped it with the front of her shirt, like she used to when I was real small.

"What a day this has been, huh? How about we go have our hamburgers? And we'll talk more," she said. As she moved, there was a crackling noise underfoot. She looked down.

"It's Frank's, Mom," I said. "Leave it be. Nit tried to tell me this was a sad place and not to dig it up, but I didn't listen to her." My voice cracked right down the middle. Burned my throat.

"What is it?" Mom said, nudging the box gently with her foot.

"It's his old life."

Chapter 38

We didn't see Maxey for hours. Mom tried to get her to come out and eat, but she wouldn't. Then she tried to go in and talk to her, but Maxey moved the dresser in front of the door. Mom finally left her dinner on a plate in the hallway.

"But what if she doesn't ever come down?" I asked, looking up toward the stairs.

"Well, if she doesn't come down tonight, you can sleep in the office on the couch. But I bet she will."

Mom and I were sitting in the living room together, looking at some of her old college pictures. There were a lot of them of her and Frank together. I think she pulled out her albums because she was trying to work things out in her head too. Just like Maxey.

Mom looked down at me and touched my cheek. "You still have green freckles."

"I know," I said, reaching up and rubbing them. "They won't come off. I even tried some Ajax."

"Effie! Never use Ajax on your face! What kind of pen did you use?"

"One from your coaching bag."

"No wonder," she said. "Those are permanent markers I use for my team overheads. You're going to have green freckles until high school, I bet."

I sighed. "Maybe I'll just go to public school. There's probably other kids there like me."

We skimmed through more pages of pictures. It looked like Frank had been at every game my mom ever played in. "Are you upset that Frank doesn't want to be a priest anymore?" I asked.

"I don't think 'upset' is the right word. I'm so sorry it happened. I know it is tearing him up inside. Our church needs to have priests like Frank. Monsignor hopes the retreat will change his mind. I really, truly wish he could stay in the game. But they want him to be a different kind of priest than he wants to be, Ef. So, I guess I'm sad that he doesn't want to be a priest, but I'm not disappointed in him at all. You know, it would be like if my principal told me that I couldn't be a basketball coach ever again, and I had to work inside all day teaching algebra. I'd be desperately unhappy."

I thought of Sister Emmanuel, who loved being a cowgirl and a nun and was trying to be both.

"You knew when he first came here that he was thinking of

giving it up, didn't you, Mom? That's why you let him stay. You hoped you could convince him to stick it out."

She nodded. "I didn't try to convince him of anything. I tried to be a good friend and listener. He was feeling very mixed up. But in my heart, I'd hoped that he'd be able to find his way back to the church in his mind."

I thought about all the weeks he'd spent with us out in the backyard working on the labyrinth. And how he'd told me that if you have a problem and walk through it, when you come out the other end, you might have the solution. Looked like that was what happened to Frank. When he was all done building the labyrinth, he knew what the solution to his problem was. And he buried his collar and ring right there.

"Mom?" I asked, looking at one of the pictures of her and Frank laughing together. "Is there maybe a teensy-weensy part of you that's glad he's leaving the church so maybe he could be your boyfriend again someday? Not now, I mean, but maybe in the future?"

She shook her head. "Cupcake, just because Frank is leaving the church, it doesn't mean he is leaving God. That will never, ever change. And that means there probably will never be any room in his heart for a wife, or even a girlfriend."

"That's not really an answer," I said.

"Okay, Effie, you win," she said, taking her reading glasses off. "I could never date him or marry him. Ever!"

"Really?" I turned to get a full look at her. "Why not?"

"He drinks way too much grapefruit juice," she said, poking me in the side.

• • •

Mom was upstairs a long time with Maxey.

I was so pooped from the slumber party that my head was throbbing. My eyes felt like someone had thrown itching powder in them. But I was still too wired to go to sleep yet. I went into Mom's office where Frank used to sleep and pulled out another photo album, then dropped onto the couch. I kicked off my shoes and pulled the blanket over myself.

I propped the album up on my chest and flipped it open. It looked like Mom had started this one and then never got to finish it. It had a lot of pictures just shoved in the back. There were a million pictures of baby Maxey. By the time I came around, I think Mom was too tired to fuss with too many pictures of me. Plus, she had to go back to work full-time by then. And, Dad was gone all the time, too. I guess my babysitter didn't take pictures of me.

I stopped when I saw Frank's face. It was a close-up of him in his priest collar, and he was holding an itsy-bitsy baby Maxey, who had one of her fists right in his face. He had this look on him like he'd never held anything so amazing in his whole life. The two of them didn't have eyes for anyone else in the world.

I flipped over the picture to see if Mom had written anything on the back. I drew in a soft breath. The picture read, "Frank and Effie at Maxey's 2nd birthday."

It was me he was holding, not Maxey. I flipped it over and stared at it again. Stared at my miniature fist in his face. Looked at the softness in his eyes.

Nit was wrong. You can't outsmart love after all.

A soft weight landed square on top of me.

Pretty Girl!

She stood on me and looked me right in the face. Realized

her mistake. I wasn't her beloved Frank. She'd been tricked. She meowed then, pitiful, her tail quivering. She didn't know what to do next. She'd jumped all the way up and now what? I could feel her disappointment and her deep loneliness. It felt just like mine.

"It's okay, girl," I whispered, a bit nervous. I hoped she wouldn't decide to slash a big Zorro on my face or anything. She blinked at me, and I blinked back. I heard that was how cats said hello.

"Have I ever told you how pretty you are?" I said in the softest voice. "Like a movie star."

She blinked again, a bit slower this time, which I think meant "How are you?" and I blinked back just as slow. I talked some more to her in a whisper, saying Frank's name and Grandpa's and Grandma's, all the people I knew she loved. After a while, she sat on her haunches and made a little sound in her throat. Like, Don't stop. And, Let's go back to talking about what a pretty girl I am.

I eased a hand out from under the blanket and let her sniff it. I tried to pet her, but she ducked away from me. Okay, we'll take it nice and slow. I sang her one of Grandpa's favorite songs about Puff the Magic Dragon, which she enjoyed a lot. She lay all the way down then and began to wash one paw, keeping a watchful eye on me.

I showed her the picture of me and Frank and she rubbed against it. And then let me touch her head for just a moment with my little finger.

We talked for quite a bit longer after that, even though I was so bushwhacked. While she gave her bottom a thorough washing, I told her all about how I'd blown it bad with Nit, and how mixed up I'd been about Frank. Now and then she made a little chirping sound in her throat to let me know she was listening, even though she was very busy with her bath.

And that was the first night, but not the last, that my Pretty Girl slept pressed right next to me.

Chapter 39

It's pretty amazing how your whole life can flip in just two weeks. It's a good thing to remember when things feel pretty desperate. Like they did the day after my slumber party, when I discovered that Frank was a decent guy after all and I'd wasted every single day he'd been with us. I wanted a to-tal do-over with him, but you don't always get those.

But Nit gave me one the very next morning. On Sunday, I'd gotten up early, fixed Pretty Girl some breakfast, and left Mom a note. I rode my bike over to Eller's Doughnuts, then to Nit's. I stood under her window because it was too early to go to the front door. I barely had a chance to rap before she was reaching a hand out to me and dragging me up over the windowsill. She threw on a sweatshirt and went into the kitchen and made hot raspberry tea for us. We sat on the floor of her room and ate iced pink cake doughnuts, and I told her everything that had happened and how sorry I was. Her cheeks got red about that, and she said she'd forgiven me hours ago, but she appreciated the apology all the same.

She told me too that Phil had been the one to call Monsignor Finnegan and tell him where Frank was. Maxey had told Phil the name of Frank's church, and she tracked down the monsignor from there. She was hoping he'd come take Frank away so Maxey would go back to her old self. Phil missed her.

We talked a lot about Aurora and what we should do next. I told Nit about how Mom was disappointed about Frank leaving the church but not in Frank. And how she didn't try to talk him into staying or leaving. That she just wanted to be a good friend. Nit and I agreed that was the kind of best friends we wanted to be with Aurora, and not the kind that made her feel bad about leaving. Nit said maybe she could have a party at her house to celebrate Aurora's team sometime, and we could try to get to know some of her other new friends, not just Fancy.

When I got home afterward, Mom and Maxey were in the kitchen eating green pizza leftovers. I started to say something nice to Maxey, but she gave me her old look, like, "Say one word and I'll pulverize you, punk!" Mom had done a good job of getting the regular Maxey back from wherever she'd been.

They'd talked to Frank while I was gone, and Maxey got some private time on the phone with him. Mom told Frank about my taking his ruby key. He said it was the key to the tabernacle at Our Lady of Charity where they kept the Holy Communion wafers locked up. Mom told him she'd let me explain to him why I'd taken it in the first place next time I saw him. And I'd give it back to him then.

She told me I should start working on my apology to him because I owed him a T. rex–sized one. At our last Team Meeting that we had—back to the Girls Only kind—Mom started a new thing called "Great Men of the World." Every week for a while we are going to talk about really good men—they can be living or dead. People we know or not.

I keep wearing the ruby key around my neck, practicing my apology, and wondering exactly how long it'll be until I get a chance to deliver it.

• • •

I covered my head and ducked as an out-of-bounds basketball whizzed past me. Fancy came running after it and toppled over Mom and me on the bleachers.

"Easy there, girl!" Mom said, heaving her back up. "Back in the game!"

"Right, Coach!" she yelled, and hurried off.

"Would you please STOP gawking at me?" I covered my chest with my arms.

Donal grinned. "Crazy birds," he said, looking over Nit and me.

We were both wearing new medium-sized racks. We glared at him, then tried not to giggle. The fakes were my idea. You know, so that Aurora wouldn't feel like everyone was looking at just her when the three of us were together. She thought it was very funny, and she appreciated it a lot. Nit explained that we were doing it in "solidarity," and Aurora thought it was the best idea ever. She told some of her team and now they think we're pretty cool friends to have.

The three of us made a deal that we would stay best friends, no matter where Aurora went to school.

"Hey, I never thanked you for taking back my library book," I said, turning in my seat to look up at Frank.

He winked and pulled my ponytail. "You're welcome, Ef. Hey, your pal's doing great out there."

"Yeah, she is." I'd known Aurora since first grade, and I'd never seen her so happy. The kind of happy that Frank looked these days.

After his retreat, he came back to Tyler Wash and rented a house not too far from ours. He and Monsignor Finnegan and the bishop made a deal with Frank so that he could take a year off from being a priest. Sort of like Principal Obermeyer's sabbatical, only longer. Lucky for us!

He was back hard at work in our yard, putting in a pond with Stu Turner's help and building me a grown-up kind of tree house in the maple tree. Frank had also taken over the job of reading cowboy books to Sister Josephine, and the two of them were thick as thieves.

Except he wasn't a thief at all. Frank was just an ordinary guy who liked to be with God outside and make beautiful things out of messes.

Tonight, everyone was going out for burgers after the game. And by everyone, I mean *everyone*. Frank; Mom; Maxey and Phil, who were back in business; Nit; me; Aurora and her new shadow, Fancy; and Donal, who was, well, our new shadow. We couldn't shake him. He'd started to grow on me. Nit had liked him all along, I realized.

So now my list of 7 lucky things that have happened to me since I nearly got hit by lightning has three new things on it, making it 10 lucky things.

8. Principal Obermeyer came back early from her sabbatical! (She went to Aurora's house right off and apologized for how things were handled.)
9. Frank wrote a $1,000 check to the St. Dom's PE Department like he promised. Mom is trying to help get a better girls' basketball team going at St. Dom's to distract Maxey from thinking about hair all day long. Frank is helping her coach, which is a big draw for the sixth-grade girls.
10. I have a cat now that is crazy about me. Maxey is so jealous, even though she tries to act like she isn't.

And just one more thing, which I almost put on my list of lucky things on the fridge, but decided I'd better not because it's an unlucky thing that happened to someone else.

Booger Boy has fallen madly in love with Kayla Quintana! Must be her new blond hair color that covers all her black streaks. Someone started a rumor that she kissed him in the labyrinth at my party. Some of the sixth graders are even calling her "Mrs. Booger Boy"!

Bloody gift. (That means *really* superb.)

ACKNOWLEDGMENTS

With heart-swelling thanks to Wendy Lamb for giving me another opportunity to work and play in Effie's world. And for talking me through a last revision over the phone from a rental car in a hotel parking lot during her vacation. And to my infinitely talented, sapient, and lovely writing friends, Robin, Lee, Val, Ellen, and Thalia, who encourage and support me in all the right ways.

MARY HERSHEY'S LIST OF 10 LUCKY THINGS

1. She grew up in a very funny family!
2. Very cool nuns taught her how to write.
3. She was never hit by lightning, even once.
4. She didn't get in trouble for hiding all those overdue library books under her mattress.
5. She has a real-life fairy godmother.
6. She gets to live in Santa Barbara.
7. She didn't grow up and marry Booger Boy.
8. She has the nicest partner in the world.
9. She gets to meet her readers at book signings!
10. It's a secret for now....